# MY DATE WITH NEANDERTHAL WOMAN

# My Date With Neanderthal Woman

## David Galef

DZANC
BOOKS

**DZANC BOOKS**

1334 Woodbourne Street
Westland, MI 48186
www.dzancbooks.org

Published 2011 by Dzanc Books
Book layout by Steven Seighman

The following stories have been published, often in slightly altered versions:

"All You Can Eat" in *Bull: Fiction for Men*;
"The Adjuster" in *The Common Review*;
"Afternoon of a Poet" in *Pindeldyboz*;
"At the Paradise Club" in *The Texas Review*;
"Breakfast of Champions" in *Cimarron Review*;
"Crusade" in *Eclipse*;
"Food For Thought" in *Chiron Review*;
"Going Nowhere," "Natasha," and "Portrait of Duff" in *Agni Review* (online);
"Ismene" in *Sonora Review*;
"Mississippi Breakdown" in *storySouth*;
"More Than a Platonic Relationship" in *New York Stories*;
"My Date with Neanderthal Woman" in *Flash Fiction Forward* (W. W. Norton);
"The Perfect Couple" in *Prism International*;
"Question Authority" in *Fiction Southeast*;
"Still Hanging" in *Westview*;
"Waste" in *The Styles*;
"What Remains" in *Chiron Review*;
"What You Call Living" in *Flash Fiction* (online);
"Zack and the Beanstalk" in *Sojourn*;
"A Man of Ideas," "Hers," "Mistress Morpheus," and "Returns" in a limited-edition chapbook called *A Man of Ideas and Other Stories* (Noemi Press).

06 07 08 09 10 11 5 4 3 2 1
First edition November 2011
ISBN-13: 978-1936873050

Printed in the United States of America

# Table of Contents

*For Beth and Daniel, my best audience.*

# Hers

As a souvenir from her stay in Botswana, Mary Edwards brought home a slave. Her host, an effusive gentleman named Molefi Khali, pressed the gift upon her at the Gaborone airport. Despite her objections, he insisted first mildly, then strenuously, in that way she had come to recognize as the national stubbornness. "But what will I *do* with him?" she finally asked, throwing up her hands in mock despair.

"Ah, a thousand and one uses—just as in old soap cleanser ads." Molefi smiled broadly, defeating her motion with an open-handed gesture of his own. "You will see. Consider it—what? A cultural exchange." Still smiling, he got back into his car and motioned to his driver, who pulled smoothly away from the curb.

Mary was left standing with the slave, a nut-brown young man wearing a loincloth and a sort of leather jerkin, his hands crossed at the wrists, as if he were used to shackles. Dull olive eyes stared incuriously from underneath a thatch of crinkly black hair, his fleshy lips the main promontory on an otherwise flat face. He was somewhat shorter than she was, which made her feel as if she had authority.

"What's your name?" she asked, but he merely bowed. "Where are you from?" Another bow. Since all other questions elicited the same response, she shrugged, told him, "Well, you might as well make yourself useful," and handed him one of her bags. He picked up all her luggage, one suitcase in each hand, balancing the third on his head. *This will stop soon*, thought Mary, but inside the terminal, the clerk at Delta East Airlines approved the slave without any fuss, as if he were just another of Mary's bags. Since the flight was only half full, he sat in the rear of the plane, gazing stolidly ahead of him, hands in his lap, every time Mary checked.

Arriving at Kennedy International, they passed Customs without difficulty, as if the slave were invisible. By then, Mary's internal protestations of *This has gone far enough* were vying with *Let's see how far this goes*. Hailing a cab, she rode to her apartment on East 86th Street with the slave in front. Installed in her tiny living room, he sat bent-backed in the beige Modena sofa as she bustled about the bedroom, unpacking and playing back her answering machine. The only message of note, besides a waspish query from the cable service about an unpaid bill, was from Molefi. "Just so you know," unspooled the voice from Gaborone, "his name is Tiro. He doesn't understand English—you must teach him, if that's what you want—but he does know basic commands."

Mary played back the message twice to make sure she got the name right, then called Tiro from the living room. He came at once, shuffling on the deep-pile carpet. She performed an introduction long overdue, feeling supercilious, but also all of a sudden ravenous. She'd eaten almost nothing on the plane.

"Are you hungry?" she asked him, rubbing her belly and miming eating. He mirrored her motions and nodded. "Wait here," she told him, and he did. Opening the refrigerator in her cramped kitchenette, she found only a couple of pork chops and some Birds Eye peas in the freezer. Could he cook? At first he looked puzzled by her request, but she pointed to a frying pan, and he nodded and went to work. She went back to the living room to read a magazine, and thirty minutes later he emerged with a genuine meal. He had located some old potatoes in a cupboard, found her spice cabinet, and produced a stew. They ate in silence, broken only when she complimented him on the taste, licking her lips, and then pointed him toward the sink to wash the dishes.

There wasn't much to do after that. Even if they'd shared a common language, Tiro certainly didn't seem one for conversation. She spent the rest of the evening going through accumulated mail and went to sleep early, jet lagged and disoriented. Tiro slept on the Modena sofa, which fit his small frame with only a slight overhang of toes.

The next morning, Tiro was up before her, bringing her coffee and something fried from the last potato. She got herself ready and headed off to work, though apprehensive about her apartment, as if she had left a dangerous pet inside. All day at the office—she worked in public relations for Dowell & Hatch—she had to fight the impulse to rush back home. Yet at the end of the day she did a little food shopping on the way home, wondering whether Tiro would still be there when she arrived.

But of course he was. He greeted her with a low bow, and before she knew it, she was seated in a chair with her shoes off, and he was rubbing her feet. She would have protested, except that it felt so good, like a bath soaking into her. Inspecting her packages, he took them into the kitchenette and began to rattle the three pots and pan she owned. *I could get used to this*, she thought, as she spooned up some kind of fresh green soup.

A week passed, the pattern of subservience growing into routine. But she caught him gazing longingly out the window and worried about his staying indoors. She also wondered about his lack of possessions and single set of clothes, though he apparently bathed himself while she was out. So on Sunday, she went out to buy him several new outfits, including a pair of loafers to replace his shapeless sandals. When she took him for a walk in Central Park, with him in fixed proximity as if on a leash, she got some admiring glances. The new clothes had altered his look considerably, from something tribal to somebody from downtown. And his attitude had subtly altered. Was it pride of ownership or pride in being owned? That afternoon, she began teaching him certain useful English words: *wash, sew, sweep.*

To her few friends who asked, she passed him off as her houseboy. "A souvenir from Africa," she joked. She slowly taught him more complex English: *Wait here while I go into that store. Paint my nails.* And daringly one night: *Soap my back.* That led eventually to his sharing her bed, a habit that she indulged only on certain evenings. Tiro turned out to be a dutiful lover, if uninspired. Mary began to depend on him for all sorts of amenities, even on several occasions using him as a human footstool. From time to time, she thought of contacting Molefi and thanking him for such a thoughtful gift, but somehow she never got around to it. In any event, her host had been right: Tiro did have a thousand and one uses, and she was discovering new ones every day. The latest was his skill in brewing *kgadi*, a native liquor from distilled brown sugar.

During the month of September, Mary calculated, she had used Tiro as everything from tailor to silent confidant. A small man, he didn't eat much. He never complained, and showed hesitancy only when she asked him to watch certain violent TV shows with her. His English had reached a serviceable level, though he always called her "Mistress" instead of "Mary," and she didn't correct him.

Yet after six months or so, Tiro began looking worn out and started performing tasks sloppily. The first time happened when preparing dinner for three of her friends, and he tripped and broke a favorite platter. She spoke sharply to him, and he apologized profusely. Later, as the accidents piled up, his apologies began seeming perfunctory, just like his bow. Once, when he dropped a platter of chicken, she kicked him. He looked hurt, like an abused dog, but the guilt she felt only made her more annoyed. She hit him with a broom one afternoon when he hadn't swept the hallway properly. The stoic air with which he endured it grated on her.

One Saturday morning, after he overslept and missed serving her breakfast in bed, she locked him in the minuscule closet. This time he protested, but she chose not to listen. Muffled cries gave way to silence. Upon opening the closet several hours later, she was horrified to discover that he had suffocated, wedged in between the closed door, two pillows, and an old blanket. Even in death, his face bore an impassive demeanor.

After a moment's panic, she decided to put Tiro's body out on the street in one of the apartment building's gunmetal gray trash cans. If anything, he had shrunk since he had arrived in Manhattan. Inside the can, his body was neatly folded and not too heavy. It was picked up the next day.

For a while, the apartment seemed dreadfully empty, but Mary soon recovered. She met a guy at a friend's loft party, starting a short-term relationship. But she was irked that he wouldn't take orders the way Tiro had, and he definitely wouldn't perform some of the tasks she had come to expect, in bed or out.

Chalking it up as experience, she moved on. But as more time went by, she grew increasingly restless and irritable. Spring was just ahead, but it wasn't exactly romance she wanted. She kicked at the carpet and called out, but no one answered. In her datebook, she made plans for another trip to Botswana that summer.

# More Than a
# Platonic Relationship

Friday night, and Sandra was reviewing Books II through VII of Plato's *Republic*, highlighter in hand, the desk lamp angled to reach the slant-frame chair in the corner. Alternately scowling at the text and glancing out the window, she couldn't keep disquieting thoughts from intruding on Plato's description of the ideal city-state. Compulsory calisthenics and the right kind of love—what was *that* all about? Socrates was an annoying old man, that much was certain, like clever Uncle Ralph, who argued with her father over dinner and pinched her bottom when she bent over.

She flipped a page. Where did wisdom reside? Things of this world change, Socrates was arguing, so one can't learn from them. Ha. She thought about her boyfriend Frank, who hadn't altered in the three years they'd been together, probably since grade school, if his mother in Queens could be believed. He still wore baggy khakis and liked his steak medium overdone.

An iron fart blatted through the window, making her look up as if it had caught her on the chin: some truck backfiring through the intersection. 32nd Street and 10th Avenue wasn't the classiest neighborhood, but at least it was Manhattan, and there were worse stations in life than finishing up a distance-learning equivalency degree at Baruch. An old woman poked her head out a nearby window and exchanged obscenities with a skateboarder on the sidewalk opposite. True knowledge cannot come through the senses, as Professor Donovan had instructed them on his Philosophy 102 website, but at times Sandra found that a comforting thought. In that case, none of this would rub off on her.

But what about the needs of the body? Plato was strangely silent on that topic. It was already past eight, and her stomach was beginning to growl. Frank hadn't called, of course he hadn't. He'd already e-mailed her that afternoon to let her know he'd be late coming over—some overdue project at Lipsey & Miles, the architecture firm where he was interning. Of course, if it wasn't a project, it was a visit to Queens, or a basketball game downtown. She ought to have known by now, and yet. She got up, intending a trip to the whiny refrigerator, but made herself sit down again, the steep incline of the chair doing her lower back no good. $49 at Ikea, with a hard, raw-wood finish to offset the rummage-sale dresser, the lumpy gray bed. Starter furniture, as her decorator friend Marcy termed it. She tried to concentrate on the page in front of her, but the back of the chair felt as if it were beginning to part company with the rest of the frame. After ten more minutes of frowning at Plato's description of the ideal good, really ten minutes of Frank's refusing to call, she levered herself up again from the chair. A party across the street was just starting up in a boom-boom of retro-Eighties disco music, and she wasn't invited. She'd have to work on that. Her latest office temp job was due to end in another week, and the agency hadn't found anything else for her yet. Still, she knew she was talented, headed somewhere.

"I need more beauty in my life," she muttered, echoing a line she'd just read. Meanwhile, she kept herself going with thoughts of the leftover pork lo mein from the fridge and how she would fork it straight from the takeout carton. Unfortunately, all she had to wash it down with was orange juice, which didn't go well with it. And maybe, just maybe, she should wait for Frank. Plato was on to something, she was willing to admit. Maybe she should set her sights higher or something.

Should she e-mail Frank? At times he seemed like a grungy demon lover, those baby blue eyes under the dirty blond thatch piercing her soul and finding her wanting. Maybe *she* should be more beautiful, though he always said how cute her tits were. She made as if to highlight the outline of her breasts against her cutoff Everlast shirt. Too bad Professor Donovan never saw his students. Lately she had felt half-invisible, as if in a dream, especially when she walked around her neighborhood.

Which made it all the more poignant when she finally sat down again—9:15, never mind—and found her book flopped open to this passage: "As for the man who believes in beautiful things but not in the existence of Beauty itself, nor is able to follow one who leads him to the knowledge of it, do you not think that his life is a dream rather than a reality?" Since it sounded important, she dutifully highlighted it, but didn't really understand how it fit into her life. A footnote in ten-point type only muddied matters: "The Platonic Forms, which are eternal and unchanging, represent true knowledge, the only real existence."

Forms? Shit, this would be on the next test, she just knew it. Reaching over to her laptop, she brought up Professor Donovan's Plato lectures on the screen, his erudite features smiling benignly over a procession of unscrolling paragraphs. She performed a KwikSerch and found mentions in lectures two and four. Apparently, the Forms were models somehow, not just of Goodness and Beauty, but also the perfect pattern of all objects, as if there were some ideal table, the mother of all tables, an ur-table, *the pattern from which all earthly tables were taken* (Professor Donovan was on a roll). Moreover, the Forms were real, not just some abstraction. If you weren't alive to this higher reality—and this she did recall, partly from drunken discussions with Frank's philosophy major brother who'd unaccountably gone into the plumbing business— then you might as well be living in a cave, dealing with shadows instead of the real thing. But she wasn't a rationalist, just a pragmatist from Union City, trying to make it like everyone else.

Still, the whole concept was weird. She scratched her left ear, feeling a bit dizzy. To think that somewhere out there was the ideal Form of a tree or a lamp. *So why all these crappy copies?* she wondered, finally levering herself up from the chair again and almost teetering sideways to the floor. She felt lightheaded and held on to the non-ideal lamp for support. Nothing since breakfast but a small rice cake she'd brought to work. She should have eaten something a while ago. Or maybe it was the tippy chair—not even people-friendly, some model *it* was. Meanwhile, the kitchenette beckoned.

She didn't really notice the appearance of the refrigerator as she reached for the handle, but when she opened it, she was practically blinded by the light emanating from inside. Instead of the weak interior bulb, a beam as powerful as the sun illuminated an array of fresh fruit, salads, beverages, cold cuts, cheeses, breads, and pastries, like a modern cornucopia. The gleaming white-and-chrome shelves stretched toward infinity, as in a classical demonstration of perspective, the coolness frosting the outside air. The vision was so beatific that she fell to her knees. She hadn't sampled any hallucinogens since high school days, so it couldn't be that. Only after an indeterminate period of adoration—five minutes, three hours?—did she slowly rise, tentatively reaching for the Form of an apple from the perfect refrigerator.

She carried it back to the chair, which rose from its corner in a triumph of Form, its straight angles in golden ratios, the pure wood transformed into design. Settling into it, she gasped at the way it rendered support without confinement, gently correcting her posture. It made her feel upright and noble, even as it remained the template of a seat. She sat enthroned as she bit into the apple.

At that moment came a triple knock on the door, and though Sandra must have somehow undone the locks in the interim, Frank was standing right there in front of her, broad-chested and taller than she remembered him, his features radiant: the ideal boyfriend, she knew at once, and without a word he kissed her so deeply that she practically became a part of him. He carried her to the futon where they had the most amazing sex, vibrating their bodies both inside and out, her third climax so powerful that she lost consciousness.

She drifted and dreamed, sometimes encountering the Form of a typing job or still trying to appease her awful hunger, other times running from a truth that threatened to engulf her with its awful majesty. In the back of her mind was a sentence that she felt she ought to have highlighted: "If there is even a slight chance that one might be mistaken, then it is not true knowledge." In the speeded-up film that looked like life, occasionally she felt as if everyone else in the world was a puppet figure, or else she was. Slowly the scene darkened and shifted, though still blurred.

She woke up a year later, all the intervening days lined up as if in evidence, now living in a cave of an apartment in Queens with that bum Frank and a new baby. As she looked at the dingy shade in the bedroom (pulled up, it revealed a brick wall), the shadows gathered around, and everything came back to her: She had flubbed the philosophy course and never graduated, Frank was training to be an apprentice plumber, having lost his internship in circumstances he still wouldn't explain, the baby was colicky and wouldn't nap, and as Sandra reached automatically for the formula bottle on the slant-frame chair, her forearm brushed against the wooden surface and she started in surprise. It felt so cold, so hard, so real.

# What Remains

Maria got the news over the telephone that afternoon, a sympathetic but terse voice informing her that her husband Esteban Velasquez had been lost in an airplane crash. The Boeing DC-10 had simply exploded in midair over the Atlantic. The remains were unrecoverable. A terrorist bomb was suspected, though no group had yet claimed responsibility.

"Thank you," murmured Maria stupidly to the receiver, as if the bearer of bad news had heroically survived and escaped the wreckage in order to tell her. The caller went on to say something about a number to call for further information and grief counseling, but Maria heard only static in the sudden blackness that descended upon her. When she opened her eyes, she found herself seated on the floor, next to the tan espadrilles that Esteban had kicked out of his way that morning. Such a slob he was, so that dirty dishes sat on the stove, shirts and underwear lay like ghosts about the bedroom, and flecks of shaving cream and toothpaste turned the bathroom mirror into Italian marble. Yet she sobbed at the memory and even clutched one of the espadrilles to her face, inhaling the acrid scent of her husband's vanished foot.

That was when it struck her, Esteban's body gone forever—blown up into a thousand pieces, drifting and settling like confetti over the dissolving sea. Not so much as a finger for burial. At this final blow, Maria started sobbing wildly, her tears almost blinding her. After a minute, she stumbled into the bathroom for a tissue to dab at her eyes. True to form, or formlessness, Esteban had left the sink a mess. The shower curtain hung like an untucked shirt over the bathtub. But the most striking aspect was the toilet, which gave off the pungent odor of excrement. It had to be Esteban's, which always smelled of over-ripe figs (a mystery, since he never ate them fresh or dried).

She peered into the depths of the bowl. There floated Esteban's stool, a fertile brown island in a yellow sea. Here and there it was mottled black. It resembled a half-drowned log, the kind that suddenly opens with the jaws of a crocodile when examined too closely. Which was Esteban's character, in fact—sleepy but dangerous if poked. Squatting in front of the toilet, she sighed. "Oh, Esteban, you were always unmistakable." When she realized her use of the past tense, she broke into a sob again. Her husband had never left behind much except for the messy evidence of his having been in a room. Her hand automatically glided to the flushing mechanism, as she had always cleaned up after him. But as she stared at the drifting bowel movement, her hand withdrew from the lever as if burnt.

"*Madre dio*!" The last remains of Esteban, which should be treasured, or at least buried with all proper ceremony. A funerary urn, perhaps, with an inner seal of Saran Wrap against the elements. And what would the priest say, presented with such a strange request for exequies? Should he perform—how to put it?—a small black mass for this small black mass? Maria had a penchant, half-cursed, half-blessed, for humor in bleak situations.

"I will call Father Diego," she pronounced to herself. "No, I'd better visit him in person." Suddenly unable to bear the closeness of the apartment, she bethought herself into a black kerchief and her cloth coat and walked the seven blocks to the Church of San Ignacio.

An altar boy with porcelain cheeks directed her to Father Diego's office. The priest was signing documents with an impatient twist of his wrist and looked up quizzically. "Yes, Signora Velasquez?"

"It's...Esteban," she began. "He's gone."

Father Diego's eyebrows peaked like Gothic arches.

"Oh, Father, I got a call an hour ago, and they said he was blown up, and now there is no Esteban left, and all I have—." But here she stopped, unable to continue.

Father Diego rose to his customary role, consoling the new widow and offering the solace of the Lord. But when he tried to piece out the rest of the story, Signora Velasquez became semi incoherent and slightly blasphemous. Finally, through broken sentences and a few transparent gestures, she indicated her question, her problem, her hope.

"Well, well," welled Father Diego, "this poses an intriguing dilemma. I'll have to check doctrinal practice." He ruminated a moment as he patted his desk drawers absently. "Of course, what is excreted from the body is not, properly speaking, the body itself—."

"But it *was* part of him this morning!" Maria's eyes were lambent with tears. "Like the blood of Christ, when we drink the wine."

Father Diego stiffened in his cassock. "Surely, you are not comparing the bodily fluids of our Savior with the—the ejecta of a mortal man who never bothered to—"

"No, no, but *please*"—here, Maria, a bosomy woman, threw herself upon the stiffened cassock—"there must be some way of burying...honoring...what remains are there. Please come to my apartment." They stood squeezed together in the clear light of the rectory as the priest thought of precedents and possibilities. Finally, only half-disengaging himself from the distraught woman, he retrieved his soutane from the corner of his desk.

"All right," he said huskily. "I'll see what I can do."

They preserved a delicate silence all the way to the apartment building and up the elevator, a creaky cage that sighed like all the sins of the flesh. But when they reached the apartment, the door was unlocked and sounds of occupancy came from beyond the lintel. They entered to see the plump hindquarters of a woman disappearing toward the bedroom. She was humming "*Cielito Lindo*."

"Ah, I forgot." Maria clapped her cheek. "Thursday afternoon is when the woman comes to clean the apartment. Juanita!"

"In a moment," replied Juanita, her voice ricocheting around the corner. "Esteban must have left this morning, am I right? Because, you know, the bedroom is hung with flung clothes, and this bathroom—."

In an instant Maria was running for the bedroom, crying, "No, wait, stop!" Father Diego ran right after her, adroitly sidestepping a broom leaning in the doorway.

But it was too late. When Maria reached the bathroom, Juanita had just flushed the toilet, and all Maria could do was watch the sacred detritus as it was sucked into the vortex and down the pipes. For a moment, all three stood transfixed in the cramped confines of the bathroom, Juanita startled, Maria stunned, and Father Diego nonplussed.

"That was the last of my Esteban!" wailed Maria when she found her voice, pounding the water tank of the toilet. Father Diego cleared his throat and explained to the poor cleaning woman the import of what she had done. Juanita scratched herself and shook her head.

"There is no blame attached in this matter," he pronounced, holding Maria's shaking shoulders. "Your husband went to his greater reward this morning. As for what he left behind of himself"—he made a hand-washing gesture—"it has gone to the other shore." Unsure whether he was mixing paganism with Catholicism, he nonetheless continued. "'Ashes to ashes,' says the Bible, and there are many ways of interpreting these words. Your husband's last—movement has gone toward the confluence of all human wastes... in the vast sew—" (a pause before the abyss of words) "—sea where all must go. More than most men, he has indeed merged with the universe." He spread his hands for a blessing over the water tank. "He has become, in death, part of the living stream. May the rest of us be so favored. *Ora pro nobis.*" And with a ceremonial flourish, he flushed the lever twice, intoning in Latin as he did so.

Both women agreed it was a very moving ceremony. Father Diego walked back to his office, congratulating himself for solving a sticky situation, and Juanita received a consoling tip. In a short while, Maria was left alone again, the shadows of dusk creeping over the bed. Staring at the sheets, she felt as if she could stand there forever, like some saint turned to granite at the crossroad. But soon she felt an urgent distension below, what Esteban himself had always termed "the call of nature."

Almost without thinking, she moved toward the bathroom, pulled down her skirt and underwear, and sat on the white wooden seat. What seemed so basic an act now also seemed so sacrilegious, especially after Father Diego's lovely sermon.

The awful part, she thought as she lingered a moment, then pulled down the flush-lever firmly, is that I can never again relieve myself without thinking of my dear, departed husband. "Ah, well, we all have to go sometime," she murmured to the mirror, biting her lip to avoid both giggling and crying. She was only half-successful.

# At the Paradise Club

D onny Chavez was having another argument with his mother, really a continuation of the same quarrel they'd had for the past two decades, namely, why did she have to humiliate him in public all the time? "It's not like I'm five anymore." He ran a hand through his hair, thinning already in his twenties, as he maneuvered his battered Honda through the mid-afternoon traffic in East Memphis.

"Donny, Donny, Donny." His mother reached out to smooth his hair, but he shrugged her off. He still hadn't forgiven her for the latest imposition, showing up at his office temp job in the Chamford Building with a bag lunch he'd forgotten on purpose. A turkey sandwich, an orange, and a lecture delivered to him in front of the security guard.

"Ma, for Chrissake—."

The security guard, an older Hispanic man with a nightstick in a holster told him to be more respectful of his mother. What Donny said next wasn't at all deferential, and it had cost him his job. That had been on Thursday. Now it was Saturday. On Monday, Donny would have to showcase his computer skills to a new temp agency. Meanwhile he had grudgingly agreed to drive his mother to the Hickory Ridge mall to shop for some shoes. Though nearing fifty-five, she had never been comfortable behind the wheel of a car. She had learned to drive in order to deliver a ten-year-old

Donny to his trumpet lessons, then unlearned as soon as Donny received his license.

Donny drove with one-handed ease, the way his father had, though Raymond Chavez had died in a construction accident when his son was nine. Even at the funeral, Donny recalled, his mother had embarrassed the hell out of him by following him into the men's room where he was sulking and leading him back in front of all his relatives. She followed him to school; she followed him to soccer practice. She even shadowed him on the few dates he'd had, despite repeated blow-ups over what his mother called "carnal relations." That pattern had lasted for both years at Northwest Tennessee Community College. He still lived at home because he couldn't afford a place of his own. He also followed his mother into the secretarial business, except she'd worked as an office assistant at B & B Bailey's forever, whereas he couldn't advance beyond temporary status.

"Just like your father," she'd commented on endless occasions, whether at a restaurant—"Don't shovel your food in like your father"—or at his first trumpet lesson—"Your father blew like that."

Maybe something had been the matter with Raymond Chavez, a big man who'd apparently skidded through a dozen jobs before becoming foreman at Loman Builders—but who also pushed his son to walk while his wife was still dandling Donny on her knee. Raymond noodled on the trumpet in his underwear, ate peas with a knife, and seemed to have done whatever he liked. Sylvia groaned but acquiesced. There was even a hint that Donny's father had played around a bit, but his mother preserved a tight-lipped silence on the subject.

Getting his mother to act that way toward him was a trick Donny had never learned. It was as if she had become both parents after her husband's death, with twice the power and five times the level of surveillance. He tried to see the situation from her eyes, but that just made matters worse. What if she was right?

In his dreams, he was blissfully alone until his mother entered as a ghost or a girl but most often just as Mrs. Sylvia Chavez, sometimes as big as a Thanksgiving Day float. The image of his mother hovered above him, clucking, "Donny, Donny, Donny."

Now, as he idled at the intersection of Poplar and Perkins, he brought up the latest incident again. "Ma, if you just hadn't followed me to my own job—"

"But you forgot your lunch." She plucked at his sleeve.

"That's *my* business!" The light turned green, and he mashed the gas pedal, almost rear ending the red pickup in front of him.

"But I'm your mother." She placed a hand on her matronly chest. "Your business is my business. And watch your driving."

"My driving's okay, damn it." He swerved around the pickup, earning a glare from the driver, a redneck in a soiled undershirt who looked as if he'd never had a parent.

Mrs. Chavez shook her head sorrowfully. "As long as I'm your mother—"

"Pretend I don't know you! You've got to stop following me!"

"Donny, Donny, Donny." She sighed, infinitely tolerant, perpetually superior.

Looking anywhere but at her, he glimpsed a new advertisement up ahead for Beale Street, represented by a gleaming silver trumpet. He fingered his lip: he hadn't played in years. How could he with his mother's comments sounding in his ears? A block past Highland, the giant woman on the billboard of the Paradise Club beckoned to him, moving toward him in a come-hither crouch. The club was fifty feet beyond, a squat building with opaque windows and massive gold double doors. Donny had always passed the place without stopping, but this time the woman on the billboard had altered her siren song. "C'mere, baby," she crooned, "and get away from you-know-who."

Donny looked sideways at his mother. Her left arm had crept around his seat. At the mall, he knew, if he went to The Gap or to T.G.I.F.'s for a beer, she'd find some pretext to accompany him. He gritted his teeth, though she had told him that wore down the enamel. Without signaling for a turn, he zoomed across two lanes and pulled into the parking lot of the Paradise Club, where he killed the engine.

"What are you stopping here for?"

Donny got out and squared his shoulders, facing away from his mother. "I'll see you in a few hours." Was that an echo of his father's voice?

"Where are you going?" A note of anxiety he'd never heard before had crept into her voice.

"In there." He pointed.

"Are you crazy?"

"Maybe. That's *my* business." With a satisfying *shoonk*, he slammed the car door on her protesting cries. He didn't look back. He had one panicky moment at the entrance, feeling something like a goober stuck in his throat, but he swallowed and walked right in.

Inside it was cool and dark, the purple carpeting on the floors and walls outlined by thin fluorescent tubing. A bouncer stood with his beefy arms folded across his chest. Around an L shaped bend ran a Formica counter, behind which stood a languorous woman in black, chewing gum.

"That'll be ten dollars."

Donny flipped out his wallet and forked over. The ten-spot was greasy and creased, as if meant for sleazy purposes, but she slid it into her cash drawer in the space of one gum-chew.

"Check your bag," she told him.

"I don't have a bag." He made a comical hands-slapping-pockets gesture, but she didn't smile, just shrugged. The bouncer stood there impassively, as if made of meat. After a moment, Donny realized that the L-shaped alcove ended in a door with three blinking green arrows. The bass and thump of rock music seeped through like the stereo from a noisy neighbor. Donny took a shallow breath, coughed once, and entered.

The interior was a well-upholstered cave, with an oval stage and a woman pole dancing near the center. As Donny made his way forward, tables mushroomed in his path, flanked by wall sofas and ringside seats. Several men lounged with their legs apart, smoking and drinking, as they watched the woman onstage slowly remove her halter top and fling it precisely within a foot of the edge. She was doing a bump and grind to Madonna's "Material Girl." Her breasts were teacups on her chest, the dark nipples like eyes, and she was staring right at Donny when he collided with a table. Losing his balance, he collapsed into a chair and barked his shin. As if on cue, a cocktail waitress at least as foxy as the woman onstage swished over to take his drink order. She wore a midnight blue bustier but managed to look businesslike at the same time.

"What'll it be?"

"I don't really want anything." He wasn't even sure he wanted to remain here, but he was pleased to be in an absolutely motherless location.

"One-drink minimum. House rule."

"Oh." He peered around to see what the others were having. Mostly beer, it looked like. "Bud Light?" he asked.

"You got it." She glided away and came back a moment later with a bottle. "Six-fifty."

Donny figured he was being bilked but also knew he had no choice. He dug into his jeans for another ten-spot and, on impulse, told her to keep the change.

"Thanks, sweetie." The waitress flashed a neon smile at him and squeezed his arm.

Onstage, the dancer was down to a pearlescent white thong that she stretched and snapped. Her legs extended in a muscled V as she held onto the pole and slowly slid to the stage. Then she crawled forward to the edge of the oval, her ass like an overturned heart. A few of the patrons shoved dollar bills into her thong. One man held a rolled-up five-dollar bill in his mouth and let her pick it up between her breasts. Unconsciously, Donny leaned forward.

"Care for some company?" A blonde in an extremely abbreviated green evening gown placed a hand on his chair. She looked like an upscale version of all the girls who'd evaded him in college. The only one who'd gone out with him was Myrna Ramsey, no great looker, and she'd done it for help on a computer project. His mother, of course, had demanded an introduction and praised Donny's qualities. "My boy Donny," she'd elaborated, pinching her son's arm, "is good husband material." Myrna hadn't taken the hint. Instead, she'd dropped out of NTCC her second semester and was now waitressing at Houlihan's.

"You and your mother, you're like an out take from the 1950s," she'd told him.

"You should have known my father!" he wanted to shout, but didn't. He hadn't had a date since, unless you counted a couple of coffees with a data processor at work—at his former work, he amended. It seemed like ten years ago.

All this washed back to him in an acid reflux of anger spiked with regret. But when he turned his head, the blonde was still standing two inches away, her waist at the level of his nose. "You okay, honey?" she whispered, bending over him.

Donny gazed up at her. Her inflated chest heaved as if sighing all by itself. Beyond her, the woman onstage slapped her own butt, like a naughty girl chastising herself. On the table in front of him was a cold beer. Not a mother in sight. He looked up at the blonde and smiled. "Never better."

The blonde's smile widened into a bright chasm. "That's nice. Care for a table dance?"

It sounded like an invitation to a waltz, but Donny wasn't so naïve. He watched TV. "How much?"

"Twenty dollars."

He hesitated. On one hand, he'd already dropped that amount already. On the other hand, the boldness of the question unsettled him. On yet another hand—he was running out of hands here—what the hell did he expect? He thought about his life up till now, singularly uneventful. In three months he'd be twenty-five. He looked around the room. Two football player types were leering at a balloon-breasted black dancer waiting in the wings. A fat man in a gray business suit was motioning for a third beer. What entitled these guys to what they got?

Donny reached for his billfold again. "Okay," he told her. "But make it good."

"Sure." The blonde caressed the twenty from his hand and tucked it into a slit in her dress, bending over him so he could see the bill disappear. Mounting the table on her knees, she writhed toward and away from him, slowly slipping from the dress like a snake shedding its skin. It fell to the carpet without a sound. Underneath she wore a black bra and thong. Donny instinctively pulled back, but she reached out to bring his head nearer. Up close, her breasts looked like a hilly landscape above the valley of her torso. She arched over the chair, embracing the air around him, releasing a scent of jasmine and a little musk. After a few passes, she reached behind to remove her bra. Her breasts popped out an inch from his face, and one nipple rubbed his cheek. Donny sighed hugely, his hands dangling at his side, unable to move. She extended one leg and, without losing her balance, stroked his side with her thigh. She pivoted to show him the thinnest part of her thong. He half-closed his eyes, the better to drown in her. She had just bent over to demonstrate the flare of her buttocks when he heard a familiar voice calling his name.

"Donny, where are you?"

At the sound of that voice, he bolted forward—right into the dancer's ass. She tried to grab onto something but was knocked to the carpet. She swore something that Donny couldn't quite hear. With her off the table, Donny now saw his mother wandering past the stage. She seemed overdressed in her blouse and skirt, her handbag clamped under her arm. Outlined by a pink spotlight, she looked like an out-of-place cartoon.

"Donny?" She shaded her brow with one hand, trying to make out the few figures seated in the darkness. "I know you're here. Listen—"

"Down in front, lady!" One of the football players waved impatiently at her.

She turned to face him. "I'm looking for my son. His name is Donny. He came in here a while ago."

The other football player guffawed. "Hey, Donny, your mom's here!"

The bouncer burst through the entry door, trundling forward on thick legs. "Hey, lady, you ain't paid!"

The amplifiers kept blaring "Spinning Wheel," but the stage light, now fuchsia, seemed to shift toward Sylvia Chavez. She turned back to the bouncer. "I told you, I'm just here to check on my son."

The bouncer shook his head. "Everybody pays."

The fat man in the business suit held up two fives. "I'll cover that."

The bouncer looked in the direction of the black curtain panels that parted whenever a new girl came onstage. A heavy-faced man in a sports jacket stood by the curtain, and he gave the bouncer an almost imperceptible nod. The bouncer swiped the bills and trundled back to the entrance.

Most of the men had already swiveled their heads back to the stage, where the black dancer was straddling the pole like a love-starved fireman. Donny's blonde had already wriggled back into her dress and flounced through the curtains. Donny was trying to hunch in back of his beer bottle, but it was like hiding behind a microphone. His mother spotted him and headed straight for his table, handbag swinging.

"Donny, Donny, Donny." The low lights emphasized her heavy bust.

For a moment, Donny wished he were the size of a dollar bill and could be stuffed inside a dancer's bra. He covered his face.

But there she was, solid as a pillar beside him. She placed her handbag on the table, next to his half-drunk beer. A lecture was coming, he could feel it. "Look, Ma—"

"Is that really your *mother*?" The fat man had gotten out of his chair and was making his way back to their table. Donny still had his hand over his face, but he peered at him—and at the dancer onstage—through his fingers.

Mrs. Chavez drew herself up to her full 5´5˝. "I'm Donny's mother, yes." Then she remembered elementary politeness. "Thank you for paying my admission."

The man, who seemed to be of the old school and maybe a little drunk, took her hand and kissed it. "Listen, you must be some woman." He glanced in the direction of Donny, whose fingers had slid from his face. "It's tough taking care of a boy like that."

Mrs. Chavez sighed meaningfully, her bosom rising and falling for all the errant offspring of the world. "It is a chore at times, I'll admit." Placing her hand proprietorially on her handbag, she claimed the space around her. She leaned toward Donny. "Well, aren't you going to offer us a seat?"

Donny spread his hands helplessly. "Be my guest."

"Manners." Another sigh from Sylvia as she settled into the adjoining seat and motioned for the fat man to join her. Donny edged his chair away as the cocktail waitress swished toward them.

"I know what you mean." The fat man eased himself into his appointed chair with a groan to match Sylvia's sigh. "Look, what are you drinking? My treat."

Sylvia favored him with a smile that said, *You shouldn't, but I will*, clearly intended to flatter the man while shutting out her son. "Okay, then. A sloe gin fizz."

In a minute, she was sipping her drink and talking with the man about the cares of parenthood. His name was Arnold Lansky, and he was in the dry cleaning business. She referred to Donny in the third-person, as in, "He doesn't seem to realize that he can't just do anything he wants to," and, "Of course, he never thinks that I have needs, too." She punctuated this last comment with such reproach that Donny, who'd managed to put almost six feet between himself and his mother, froze in his chair-maneuvering.

Before Donny could defend himself, the fat man chimed in.

"That's right, young man. Your mother's a capable woman. You—you should be grateful, you know that?" He placed a paw protectively over her hand.

Sylvia patted the sleeve of his jacket. "Thank you, Arnold." She didn't remove her hand from under his but instead continued to talk about Donny as if he weren't there. Ungrateful offspring, office work. Donny couldn't hear everything over the music but understood that the subject was shifting again. "Other men, no. But my husband never took the trouble to—." She stopped, looking speculatively at Donny, as if wondering whether he was old enough to hear such confidences.

Arnold caught on instantly. He scowled paternally in Donny's direction. "Listen, why don't you wait outside while your mother and I finish our chat?"

Donny was about to protest when his mother nodded. "Go ahead, Donny. Just wait in the car, okay? As long as I know where you are."

Donny opened his mouth, then shut it. His face felt the same shade of fuchsia that lit up the stage. Finally, with a shudder that passed through his whole body, he dragged himself out of his seat. The sound system was playing "Beat It." As he left the area, his dancer, the woman in the green dress, was now onstage, peeling down again. Catching sight of Donny as she slid around the pole and snapped her thong, she gave him the briefest of waves.

# Mistress Morpheus

After I lost my wife, I couldn't sleep for weeks. Night after night, I'd lie on my side of the bed, staring hopelessly at the walls and ceiling that enclosed me like a gray vault. Even the strongest tranquilizers didn't work, reducing me to a stupor without actually knocking me out. I couldn't seem to relax my brain, which had turned into a clenched fist. In desperation, I called an escort service. "Send me someone with a soothing touch," I told them.

She came at nine, wearing a trench coat the color of dusk. Tall and full breasted, she had eyes ringed in shadow, or maybe it was just the poor lighting in my bedroom. When I told her what I wanted, she nodded as if it were perfectly obvious. "Just lie back," she said, "and leave it to me." With my head on the pillow, the scene of so many nocturnal defeats, she reached out with long white fingers and began to rub my temples. Her touch was gentle yet firm, erasing whatever resistance I'd built up. As she moved on to smoothing my brow, my eyes began to shut involuntarily. Perversely, I wanted to prolong this drowsy pleasure, but my limbs had turned to lead. My last memory was of a kiss, the merest brushing of her lips against my forehead, before I fell into a dreamless sleep.

When I awoke some ten hours later, she had gone. I felt tremendously refreshed, and for the next few days managed to get to sleep simply by replaying her touch in my mind. But soon enough, the memory faded, and I lay tense in bed. I waited half a week longer, then made the call. This time, I asked specifically for the same woman.

She arrived at nine again and led me over to the bed without saying a word. Once more, her fingers worked their magic, untying the knots in my life, the scene ending in her goodnight kiss. And again and again, as I began to call her weekly, her ministrations now a necessity rather than a caprice. We rarely talked, and she seemed to desire nothing other than putting me to sleep.

Yet eventually her mere touch began to lose its potency, relaxing but not enough to push me over the edge. Sensing this, she took my head into her lap, bending over with her long dark hair haloed around me. Cushioned against her thighs, I felt aroused but also semi-submerged, as if pressed into another world. I looked up— her breasts blocked out the overhead light—and sank into sleep as she brushed her lips against my cheek.

The head-in-lap routine was effective for weeks, but it, too, began to lose its power. The next time, she simply took my head in those strong hands and pushed it down to her chest. The swell of her breast was like an endless curve as she guided my mouth to her dark areola. The first sucking filled me with heavy warmth, and I slid into unconsciousness soon after she shifted me to her other breast. I barely registered the final kiss and slept like a baby.

Hiring a woman even on a weekly basis was expensive, but I had long ago given up computing its cost. The escort service had my credit card information, and the visits continued every Friday. When nursing lost its pull, she forced me down on the bed and French-kissed me, somehow entangling our tongues, and slowly sucked me into her. I felt myself swallowed into her dark core. I awoke the next morning, alone and afraid. Another time, her arm snaked around my neck and cut off my air. By the time I realized what was happening, it was too late.

I called the escort agency to complain, but was told that the woman no longer worked there.

Still she came. When I protested, she shushed me with one tapered finger. I struggled, so she straddled me. When I locked the door against her, she somehow managed to get inside. Friday at nine, I wait helplessly in my bedroom. Whatever she did last week was deep and lasting. Here she is, having whispered through the door. She pauses a moment, smiling faintly. Then she holds out her arms and draws me into her embrace.

# The Perfect Couple

Joe and Norma never fell into the usual marital spats about free time and sex and money and power. Nor did they wrangle much over where to eat out (they both favored French bistro fare), what to do on Sunday afternoons (museums or movies), or how to furnish their West 75th Street apartment (retro pop on brick walls, Italian art deco furniture). Instead, they quarreled constantly, with the monstrous fidelity of abiding love, over who suffered more and how.

"Christ, it's been a rotten day," Joe said Friday evening as he came home with his jacket over his shoulder, like the dashing lawyer he once was and still hoped to be. After making partner at Dougalby and Hache seven years ago, he had begun to subtly sag. He unloaded a bag from Fairway's that included mesquite-smoked turkey, twin baby baguettes, and arugula, all loosely comprising the theme of dinner. He announced each purchase in turn as if it were an important item of evidence, then returned to the motif of his day. "First, Alan, that pain in the ass, didn't prepare the backup we needed, then Marty somehow landed us with the wrong briefs, but that's nothing—"

"Compared with the trials *I've* been through," announced Norma, spreading her arms like a despairing diva rather than the graphics artist she was. She worked for a firm called Le Logo, which valued her at precisely her level of ability, which made for constant friction. "I had to run off five different versions of that chicken-head sketch before Arnold would let me show it, and then—"

"*Rrraaanh!*" cried Desmond, sinking his claws into the tan armrest just above Norma's tanned arm. Married almost a decade, Joe and Norma had long ago decided against a status-child in favor of a cat, the only animal who could make even more insistent claims on their attention than they did and so draw them a little out of themselves. Desmond, a baroque-looking Manx with a gray-and-white coat, had his own chair, his own feline ego, and maybe even his own sex life if Norma hadn't insisted on having him fixed several years earlier when the furniture began to smell like ambergris. Now he spent his days padding around the apartment and sunning himself in his chair by the window. For dinner, he received an absurdly generous portion of smoked turkey and some Highland Farms clotted cream in a bowl. Norma made a sort of salad, and the two humans dined in comparative silence. The rest of the night passed in magazines and a Thin Man video.

On Saturday morning when Joe was out running, Norma stared at herself in the bedroom's full-length mirror for a while. The apartment had two other large-scale models, in the bathroom and by the front of the walk-in closet, but the one in the bedroom, through the subtlest warping, flattered her figure. If only she weren't so damned tired. She felt pale and looked bruised, or was that the other way around? She spent the next ten minutes brewing coffee for herself and her weekend athlete. Joe liked it strong and she liked it weak, but today she felt somewhat accommodating and made it medium strength for them both. Desmond got a little skim milk in a saucer. *Look at me*, she communicated to Joe by telepathy on his return, not yet willing to come right out and say how crappy she felt. *Be more sensitive to my needs.*

When Joe came out of the shower, he stretched hugely. "Look at me," he commented, "already yawning this early."

"I hope to hell I feel better on Monday," Norma mumbled into her pillow that evening. But she didn't. Sunday was just as bad, and getting up for the workweek was like carrying around heavy carpeting on her arms and legs. Her whole body ached, and she felt—what was the word her British friend Dorothy used?— *rheumy*. She decided to stay in bed.

"I've god a code," she told Joe as soon as he came home, and he nodded in confirmation.

"I was worried about you," he told her unconvincingly as he proceeded to describe his harrowing day: more missing briefs and underling problems. Still, he did heat up some broth for her and watched approvingly as she spooned half of it up, leaving the rest for Desmond. She took some heavy cold medication and dropped into bed at nine.

But the cold didn't go away, and soon Joe began getting impatient with the sickness routine. Or, as he put it irritatingly, "Aren't you sick of being sick? I know I am." When she began coughing up green gunk the second week, Joe insisted she call Dr. Schlansky, a balding gastroenterologist who put on an avuncular GP act for his nostalgia-ridden patients.

"Now, there, young lady, " he told Norma, who felt like ninety, "what seems to be the problem?"

"I don't know...." Despite her confessional bent, with doctors Norma was of the "don't ask, don't tell" school of medicine, under the illusion that she was basically okay until admitting she was ill. It even bothered her to bring in an appliance and have the repairman tell her what the problem was.

"Well, let's just check under the hood." Dr. Schlansky stethoscoped her chest, depressed her tongue, and gave her a prescription for good old-fashioned tetracycline. "May be something bacterial. There's a lot of that going around this season," he told her.

Norma was adept at popping pills. She swallowed her antibiotics daily with a swig of Evian, and after a week the symptoms disappeared. Then Joe came home sick. He said he felt achy and lay on the sofa with Desmond purring against his back. Norma fussed over him a little, bringing him aspirin and cappuccino in bed, which was more her idea of a good time than his. Joe was no more into denial than Norma but didn't like what he called "coddling his illness," which he felt was making concessions. He even tried to keep up his racquetball.

"My impatient patient," murmured Norma possessively, taking his temperature and announcing that he had a low-grade fever.

"Low-grade. My God, can't I even have high-quality symptoms?" He looked rumpled in his blue-striped pajamas, forming a sort of nest by his groin, into which Desmond snuggled. "I haven't got time for this."

But the achiness persisted, funneling into a lump under his left armpit. And even though he self-diagnosed it as a blocked sweat gland, he dutifully went to his doctor, a gangly internist named Behrens, on the principle of what's sauce for the goose is sauce for the gander, though who'd first said that, Norma or himself, he couldn't remember.

Dr. Behrens gave him a full physical check-up, peered at Joe's left armpit, said it was probably an infected gland, and put him on azithromycin. The achiness mostly dissipated, though the swelling didn't recede much. When he went out to run on Sundays, he felt clunkier, as if running in combat boots, but couldn't prove anything since he'd stopped timing himself after making partner. That Norma said nothing about it bothered him. He waited vainly, in vain.

As Norma's analyst once explained to her, women's narcissism was based chiefly on appearances and a wish to be adored, whereas men's narcissism was founded more on performance and a need to be admired (Norma digested all this but soon forgot it, as she did with almost everything her therapist told her). Thus, Norma would continually tell Joe, "God, my hair looks so mousy," inviting a tricky-to-negotiate cross between sympathy and spirited disagreement. And Joe would complain about his slowing down but grow peevish if she concurred with him. When he resumed his racquetball on Tuesday and Thursday nights, Norma joined an evening life-painting class downtown and began having long coffees afterward with a Cooper Union crowd. They contemplated buying a 1960s Eames chair for the living room but couldn't agree where to put it. Time passed desultorily until September, when the ficus leaves began to swirl about the sewer gratings, and Norma came down with something upper respiratory, which this time really lingered.

"You look pale again," Joe accused her.

"I know." She coughed into her latest bouquet of tissues. *I suffer in silence,* she radioed him. *Tell me how I look like a doomed heroine from a nineteenth-century novel.*

He shook his head. "This is aging both of us."

"Shut up, Joe," she told him.

"It's understandable you're upset. I felt that way when I was sick." He gave her such a sweetly comprehending smile that she wanted to kick him.

"This isn't going away," he told her after three weeks. "If you love me, you'll go see Dr. Schlansky again."

"Your white cell count is over 90,000." Doctor Schlansky's lips, usually as wide-open and mobile as a comedian's, compressed into two bloodless lines. "I'm sending your sample to a hematologist."

"Which means?" asked Joe that night. He paced in a circle bounded by their Afghan throw rug. "What does he think it is?"

"I don't know, I don't know, I hope it's not—that." Norma had contracted into a fetal ball on their newly acquired Eames chair, holding onto her feet and rocking mournfully. Desmond batted a catnip mouse in her direction, but she simply wasn't interested. Getting through the week was like crouching under a ruined ceiling, waiting for a large chunk of plaster to fall on her head. Joe kept telling her how upset he was. When she finally went back to the doctor's office—no results over the phone—she took baby steps all the way.

"Look, I'll be as honest as I can with you." Dr. Schlansky passed a hand over his thinning gray hair, and suddenly Norma realized how her doctor had aged since she'd started seeing him seven years earlier. "We've checked the blood smears. They show a pattern of myelocytic leukemia—we're not sure how advanced. We need to do a bone-marrow extraction for that. Now, we're going to be aggressive about this," he continued helplessly as Norma started sobbing. He offered her a tissue from his desk, and in taking it she clutched his hand up to the wrist. After a while, he gently disengaged himself and sent her to the nurse to set up another appointment.

"Oh, God, I can't believe it—my darling!" Joe held her so hard that she felt him almost pass through her. He acted both consolatory to her and angry at the world, and he tiptoed around the apartment performing little kindnesses for her until she told him to quit it, she wasn't that far gone. But when the bone-marrow results came back, she locked herself into the bathroom and wouldn't come out for hours. Staring at herself in the mirror, she imagined herself already wasted away. "At least I don't have to worry about going on a diet," she told her reflection, her laugh a frog's croak. She wanted to go to Argyle, a cute little *boîte* in the East Twenties, but the drug regimen Schlansky had put her on didn't leave her much of an appetite, and she ended up vomiting instead and ruining a Prada blouse. The chemo was dripped in through an IV, but it seemed to hit like a wave.

Joe played the role of ministering angel for a while, showing unsuspected creativity in his ministrations: he put bouquets in the armholes of her jacket in the closet, and he even half-trained Desmond to half-fetch Norma's slippers. "I know you're suffering, too," she told him, kissing his stiff upper lip.

"Listen, you're strong, and I know we'll beat this thing." It wasn't necessarily what he believed, but it had the right tough-guy edge. He put his whole ego into it. He tried to remind himself that when she snapped at him, it was just her illness speaking, even after she pronounced, "Fuck you, it's me, Norma." He cut back on his racquetball nights to attend to her and felt he was attaining the status of a saint. The needier she became, the stronger he felt.

It couldn't last. Two months into her treatment, he announced, "I'm bushed," to Desmond, who had taken to eyeing him suspiciously as if he were a faux Joe. His fatigue didn't disappear but grew to encompass his whole day. It felt like another low-grade fever that wouldn't go away, and his left armpit ached again. Back to Dr. Behrens, who clucked his tongue and said they'd do a biopsy. Joe paced the living room at night. "Biopsy, biopsy—why do I hate that word?" Norma bit her tongue for his sake and bought seven different wigs to cover her growing baldness.

The diagnosis of lymphoma (non-Hodgkin's, metastasized to the chest) was delivered by the end of the week in a consultation room with the lights dimmed, as if in recognition of the dismal news. Behrens put his hands on Joe's shoulders, like coaching a punch-drunk fighter before the final round.

"Look, it's not the end of the battle. We've still got some firepower to combat this invasion." Usually Joe admired Behrens's military metaphors, but today they struck him as overdone. He viciously kicked at a row of trash cans on the way home until the super came out and told him to beat it.

Norma held him tight, murmuring, "Oh, Joe," repeatedly. She found the rhythm soothing. Norma had read about Florence Nightingale when she was a girl and began to really get into it. In the days that followed, she was so sympathetic that he suspected a misery-loves-company motive, though he couldn't quite bring himself to say that. Instead, he let himself be given a temple rub and a foot massage. All Sunday the three of them, with Desmond in the middle, lay in bed and made up games to pass the time. Norma won the ceiling-shadow labeling contest, but Desmond beat them both in hide-and-find the catnip mouse.

"I'm still going to work," announced Joe the next day, stuffing three fat folders into his briefcase. "I won't let this take me over." When he got to his office, no one treated him any differently, and at first he was pleased.

*Arnold told me to take off as long as I wanted,* mused Norma. *Do I really look that bad?* She spent over an hour in front of the closet mirror, scheduled a four-thirty facial at Maxine's, and appeared at Le Logo a little before lunch. She soon became absorbed in her latest project, a scholarly-looking jack rabbit for a speedy copy service. She had the impression that everyone was tiptoeing around her but didn't feel she could say anything. As for telling other people, both she and Joe were single children, and only their mothers were still alive, in twin nursing homes three miles apart. Joe guardedly informed two of his colleagues *cum* racquetball partners, and they surreptitiously told a few others. That meant he was treated more deferentially at work, a subtle shift—until a secretary sobbed how sorry she was to hear that he had lymphoma, and that night he played his last game of racquetball, weakened but vicious and uncontrollable. "Joe's final game," he narrated it to himself, distorting the score in his memory.

Norma's art friends whispered how sorry they were, and behind her back how sorry a sight she had become. Norma thought briefly of herself as a work in transition, but performance art wasn't her métier. She took to bringing home what she called her Scarred Nudes, a series of naked women with tumorous black splotches in strategic areas. Dr. Schlansky had vetoed a bone-marrow transplant because there was no match available. "I am truly unique," she consoled herself.

A few weeks later, she and Joe agreed to rendezvous after work at Sakura, a sushi place in the East Fifties. Joe, who had just started on a new drug regimen, ordered a tekamaki plate that he couldn't finish. Just to be polite, Norma got plain white rice and with one chopstick pushed around the pickles that came with it. They sipped green tea and tried to commiserate with each other.

"I know you feel drekky," said Joe.

Norma thought he was referring to how she looked. "Well, you've got to be run down, too. It's taken you half an hour to attack that tekamaki." She leaned closer, her pale face and shadowed eyes Munch-like. "Offhand, I'd say it's winning."

Joe viciously stabbed the remaining half of his food with a chopstick and said hoarsely, "Let's leave."

Three months later came a roller coaster of remissions and false hopes. "I feel like *me* again!" announced Norma brightly, wondering aloud whether she should join a gym. "My self image is back."

"I'm glad to hear it," mumbled Joe. When he complained, she let him, but what good did that do? Even Desmond, with his finicky feline soul, seemed to treat him with forbearance. What hit him most was his inability to perform, whether in bed or in court. And here was Norma chattering about a health club. He let Dr. Behrens switch his medication and hoped for a change—better or worse, he didn't care.

The new drugs took a while to make themselves felt, but they kicked in just as Norma fell ill again. Joe slowly reacquired his energy and even wondered whether he could beat some of his former racquetball partners again. *That's the old Joe*, he sang to himself. Meanwhile, a deep-seated infection lodged in Norma's left lung, and she was prone to coughing spasms that lasted from the couch to the bathroom. She began to bruise as easily as an over-ripe peach, an unkind comparison that Joe made one night after noticing the mottled skin on her forearms.

"Damn it, Joe, if you knew how I felt—"

"But I *do* know how you feel—"

"No," she declared. "Lymphoma's not as bad as leukemia."

He stuck his mottled tongue out at her. "It's worse."

She threw up her hands. "All right, it's different."

"*Vive la différence*." He would have pursued the sarcasm, but Norma snatched that moment to have one of her coughing fits, dramatizing her illness.

High on prednisone, one of the immuno-suppressant mainstays in his new arsenal, as Dr. Behrens called it, Joe succumbed to a stomach bug that he might have otherwise fought off. "Messy, messy," chided Norma as she stepped from the shower around her retching husband. Joe rolled his eyes at her, she rolled hers back, and they erupted into a bile-black laughter that they both cherished for the rest of the day.

"A pact, okay?" said Norma the next morning. She was industriously applying foundation to hide her sallow complexion. One of her discarded wigs lay splayed on the toilet seat cover as if covering a giant white groin. "You don't comment on my appearance, and I won't make any cracks about yours."

"What's the matter with the way I look?" demanded Joe, who'd just finished checking his urine for blood. Not that it was supposed to be one of the symptoms, but he worried anyway.

"Nothing, dear." She smiled in a way that seemed to crack her face in half, then pecked him on the cheek. "We're both perfect, okay?"

Joe forced a grin. "Right. Every day in every way, we're getting better and better. Our mantra for the day."

No one asked Desmond what he thought.

One Monday evening, Norma dragged herself home from what was left of her job at Le Logo at around the same time that Joe limped back from lawyering and Fairway's. Hearing the *clunk-clunk* of his wingtips up the stairs, she wished for a moment that the sound would just continue upward, past the threshold of the door. No one to judge her, no one to detract from her suffering. But the key came out of the jingly pocket to fumble in the lock, and Mr. Sick walked in.

"Took me half an hour to get through the subway crowd," he groaned, a little more theatrically than necessary.

"That's nothing," she practically cackled. "I had a dizzy spell after lunch that floored me."

"Anyway, I made it to the store." He hoisted his limp plastic bag heroically. "I got smoked turkey and some hothouse tomatoes—"

"*Yukk.* Even the thought of food—"

"I know, I know, but we've got to eat."

"You do it, then."

"I don't feel so great, either, you know."

They compared recent symptoms: his night-sweats versus her infections, her bronchial troubles as opposed to his endless aches.

"I win," she announced with as much triumph as her blocked air passages could muster.

"The hell you say!" He intended to kick the table but connected with Desmond instead, who hissed as he fled into the living room. At night, both had dreams of impossible health, usually at the expense of the other, symbolized in Joe's versions by a coal furnace of guilt. Norma dreamed of endless fields marked by gaping pits, a man stuck in each of them.

They pondered the idea of couples counseling, going so far as to get a recommendation for a grief therapist. "But I don't see much of a future in it," Norma joked. The leukemia had spread to her bones, and Dr. Schlanksy had begun to mumble. Joe's condition had hit a new low, stabilized by yet another drug therapy. Dr. Behrens was sticking to his military metaphors but talking more of conditional surrender. Joe could barely walk. Desmond was regretfully packed off to a friend of Norma's who already had seven cats and wouldn't mind one more.

They had checked into the Waldorf on their fifth anniversary, which now seemed in retrospect like some mythical faraway country. As their tenth anniversary loomed in the iron cold of February, they decided to go away again.

"I guess you pay on the way out," whispered Joe as he was wheeled into the elevator. He insisted on pushing the button himself, which made him feel more in control, even though Norma wanted to push it for the same reason.

"Ask about the room service," cracked Norma wheezily. When Joe was wheeled out on the tenth floor, Norma blew him a kiss but stayed inside. By mutual agreement, they would be on separate levels. It had simply grown too difficult to keep competing. But Norma was determined to out-suffer him, and she visited her husband for two weeks as his vision darkened and his jaw slackened. They talked about themselves like two tape recorders slowly running down in an empty room. Every once in a while, when they paused to acknowledge each other, they could be tender.

"You look in rare form," she informed him, knowing he liked that phrase.

"You're not so well done yourself." He grinned like a skull.

During Joe's last few days, in and out of lucidity, he talked about torts, and he died with his arm upraised as if to connect in a final racquetball shot.

Norma survived him by less than a day, her mind numbed with painkillers and filled with floating shapes that wouldn't stay still long enough for her to paint them. *I'm still here*, she thought right near the end. But when she turned to tell Joe, he wasn't there, and that just killed her.

# A Man of Ideas

Beware the impractical man, a passel of schemes in his head—
"I will invent a combination shoe-sneaker called the seeker,
which always finds its way home"—with a wild glint in his eye—"I
will arise at 5:30 every morning to read Dante and learn Italian
that way." These men turn horribly impractical when they become
fathers—"Let the children eat nothing but grapes for a month to
improve their bowels!" Their wives either cherish or divorce them,
and their sons and daughters, in reaction, often grow common-
sensical and a little costive.

Behold Bernardo Lazar—note the *o* after Bernard, one of his
many inventions—Bernardo, with his corkscrew curls flanking
his balding pate and a stooped posture from inclining toward his
many ideas. His wife Samantha worked as a secretary to eke out
Bernardo's salary as a janitor. His children Thomas and Thomasina—"interchangeable names!" cried you-know-who—were aged
eight and ten and attended the local elementary school, with spo-
radic tutoring in astronomy and Dante.

It was the 1950s. The Lazar home at the end of Primrose Drive
was a testament to Bernardo's projects, from the scrap metal heap
in the back yard—"what we need is a smelter"—to the blackened
windows on all sides—"helps to conserve energy." The front yard
would have boasted a grove of orange trees, but for the New Eng-
land frost that killed the seedlings. Inside was a fairly conventional

kitchen, save one or two improvements that almost exploded the oven, and now Samantha did all the cooking. The children's rooms were tiny but had half their furniture fastened to the walls at varying heights to make greater use of space. The bathroom once sported a reading rack in front of the mirror so that the children could do their homework while brushing their teeth. Thomas had actually read an entire comic book that way, but Thomasina nearly broke a tooth when the rack with her math textbook crashed into the sink.

Samantha cleared up all the wreckage, as always. The few practical ideas in the house, including a garbage chute and a compost heap, were hers. But nothing much ever stopped Bernardo's enthusiasm, just as nothing much in their lives ever improved. The past lay in fragments all over the house, the present in today's brainstorm—"dinner at breakfast!"—and the future through that glint in Bernardo's eye. Samantha no longer cherished him quite so much but had learned to endure. The children were still feeling their way along.

That is, until Bernardo's physics revolution.

"The whole world is just push and shove, but Newton decrees that for every action is an equal and opposite reaction." Bernardo made this declaration at dinner, or rather breakfast, though it was past seven in the evening. Thomasina had declined an egg and was reluctantly spooning up cold cereal. Samantha was munching on toast, leaving Thomas as the straight man.

"What do you mean, Papá?"—the last word lilted in the Italian way.

Bernardo stood up, his right forefinger inclined toward the ceiling. "I mean that when you push something—the screen door, for instance—it slams back. Or push a marble uphill, and it rolls down." The glint in his eye was back, and Samantha felt a slight headache pulsing at her temples.

"But Papá, if I push the table"—here Thomas gave their ingenious fold-up bridge table a shove, sloshing the milk in Thomasina's bowl—"it doesn't push back."

"I'll give you a push," muttered Thomasina, and did so.

Bernardo beamed. "You see? One way or another, the universe pushes back. We can make use of that."

In the moments that followed, as Samantha tried to stop the shoving match between her children, Bernardo laid out his idea for what he called Reaction Recovery. He had thought up gadgets and inventions and notions and concepts before, but never something so grand, as much a philosophy as a trick of physics. Samantha was pushed toward belief, as on so many previous occasions. That night, Bernardo didn't sleep, but instead sat at the kitchen table, feverishly covering page after page with plans and diagrams. The next day, both children were assigned RR notebooks and told to record their physical actions, whether they had visible reactions or not.

"But Daddy—"

"Papá."

"Sorry, Papá," Thomasina corrected herself. "But how are we supposed to put down every action we do? We'll be writing forever!"

"Yeah," seconded Thomas, in a rare show of sibling accord, "and anyway, writing the stuff down is another action."

Bernardo admired this convolution but couldn't let that stand in the way of scientific progress. "Okay, take it down *once*, and let that represent all writing. In fact," he realized out loud, "the notebook entries should get simpler every day. There's no need to write down any action multiple times. By day five or six, it'll be mostly repetition." His expression, so earnest a moment ago, widened into a dazzling Bernardo smile that seduced one into faith— that night could turn into day, given the right wattage, possibly powered by the energy of Reaction Recovery, just you wait and see.

Buoyed by her father's raft of confidence, Thomasina took down her seven a.m. leap from bed, her counter clockwise toothbrushing ("for odd-numbered days!"), and the raising of her carrot-juice glass to her lips. She recorded the run to the school bus and appended "movement of bus?" in parentheses. For his part, Thomas wondered whether fidgeting in math class was worth writing about. His notebook ended up as a list of activities, such as eating, walking, and going to the bathroom (including this last item pleased him immensely).

When teachers asked what the two of them were writing, both hedged and said it was "home-work," the term Samantha had told them to use for all their father's projects. It was embarrassing to be singled out, and when Jerry, the bully in Thomas's class, slung Thomas's RR notebook into a tree, it took some time and a foot of scraped skin to retrieve it. Thomasina's classmates had long ago concluded that she was nutso, but now they suspected she was writing about them, and that they found annoying. They tilted her desk and emptied all the contents onto the floor. At home, Samantha consoled them: "Your father has big plans." Bernardo quizzed them at dinner and began bringing home odd-shaped pieces of metal and wood from his janitorial job. He had always fancied himself a bit of a builder, though in fact his triplex birdhouse fell apart, and the screw-holes he drilled were often too big for the screws.

Still, he managed to construct a prototype for Reaction Recovery, starting with a spoon attached to a spring. The spring was linked to the lever of a generator-style flashlight, the kind powered by squeezing. It was true that, if you pushed the spoon hard enough, say about sixty times, a weak beam would appear for a moment. The next trick would to be to hook up the Reaction Recovery device to a hand reaching for the refrigerator door, or to a child bouncing a ball, and then find some way of storing the power—unless everyone in the neighborhood suddenly needed flashlight assistance. Bernardo stayed up late again, pondering the problem anew.

In the end, that is not important: not the five unworkable devices he dreamed up, one involving Samantha's eggbeater and a car antenna; not the sleep he lost or the patent he tried to claim, his third rejected application that year; not even the principle of

Reaction Recovery itself, which was sound as far as it went and no further, and suited Bernardo's no-waste mentality.

No, the significance of these events, I'm afraid, is that Samantha had to take on extra hours after Bernardo lost his job for pilfering, and the children were hauled into the principal's office for fiddling endlessly with their springy spoons—for which Bernardo raged impotently against the tyrannical educational system, though that didn't ease the detention given to both Thomasina and Thomas.

Even these incidents matter little compared to how the Lazar children felt a month later when Bernardo shot upright in his chair, pointing his finger heavenward, the familiar mad glint in his eyes, and Samantha excused herself abruptly, though Thomas called after her until a door slammed, and Bernardo paused only a short while before continuing with a project about giant vegetables, and not too long afterwards, someone ran away from home.

# Mississippi Breakdown

Three miles from the outskirts of Ita Bena, Mississippi, the B'nai Brith Mitzvah-Mobile began to sputter like an indignant old uncle. Behind the wheel, Manny Manheim tried to ignore the sound, but the vibration crept up the decibel scale until it began to shake the chassis of the van, and even deaf Mrs. Fishman sensed the problem.

"Maybe you should check under the hood!" she bellowed, unaware of her own decibel count.

Manny ignored both her and the engine. If he could just make Memphis, he might find a mechanic who knew what he was doing, better than the crackers out here who kept rusted car bodies on blocks in their yards. Driving around the country among the unchosen people was risky, and doubly dangerous in a region known for not welcoming Jews. But then, sighed Manny, whose parents had been Russian immigrants, what else was new?

The trip had been Rabbi Lowenthal's idea, a cross-country pilgrimage for the Elderhostel set and maybe a few able bodies from the Maccabee Assisted Living Home. Along for the ride were Mrs. Fishman, who hadn't heard a word since her loudmouth husband Lou died five years earlier in 1972 (she was also purblind); Ms. Weiner, a lifelong bachelorette who wore suspenders and a fedora; Mrs. Wolfstein, whose giant purse was stuffed with chocolate bars and butterscotch, and who tipped the scales at over three hundred pounds; and spry Mrs. Bauman, who must have been over seventy but who seemed from certain angles, particularly the rear, to have the bounce and elasticity of youth. The one man who'd signed up, an octogenarian whose children had urged him to get more fresh air, suffered a debilitating stroke shortly before departure. The seat next to Mrs. Wolfstein's, half crowded out by Mrs. Wolfstein herself, was dedicated to him.

The engine, which must also have seen better years, began to chug more evenly, calming the driver's ragged breathing. The other women, who'd been on the verge of a protest, simmered down.

Manny himself was no *poulet de printemps*, as his maiden aunt Adelaide used to say. Hired to act as chauffeur and general caretaker for the voyagers, he was on three different medications for heart and lungs, a fact he took pains to conceal from his employers. In his late sixties, over the past decade he'd had jobs as a deli waiter, a newspaper deliverer, and a taxi driver. That last job, though only part-time, had led to his current gig.

"Take good care of them," Rabbi Lowenthal had intoned, laying a heavy hand on Manny's shoulder. "And make sure you take plenty of rest stops for Mrs. Bauman. She's diabetic, you know."

Manny recalled those words over fifty drink-and-tinkle breaks later. Still, everyone had been surprisingly decent about it. And the places they stopped in, from Lynchburg to Atlanta, where the Mitzvah-Mobile had its fan belt seen to, were usually hospitable. In Tuscaloosa, they were served fried chicken and fixings by a black woman who reminded Mrs. Wolfstein of her old cleaning lady. In Biloxi, they'd been given a guided tour of the military base, where Ms. Weiner attracted the attention of a lieutenant-major.

And now this, thought Manny, slapping the steering wheel in frustration as the sputter came back worse than before. Five minutes later, with a sound like giant molars grinding, the Mitzvah-Mobile juddered to a steaming crawl. Just before it stopped, Manny managed to maneuver the van to the weed-choked shoulder.

Several seconds elapsed before anyone spoke. It was August, and as soon as the van stopped, the fan system also conked out. Mrs. Fishman, tuning in to the sudden absence of vibration, surmised that the van was no longer moving. She peered out the window like a troglodyte at the cave mouth. "Where *are* we?"

"In the middle of nowhere." Ms. Weiner snapped her suspenders with a twang.

Mrs. Bauman shook her head sagely. "Nowhere is always someone else's somewhere."

Manny pointedly said nothing. *We're in deep shit*, he was thinking, *that's where we are.* Beyond the weeds to the side of the cracked asphalt was a thick border of pine, and across the winding road a similar border. There'd been nothing else on either side for miles. The humid Mississippi air began to percolate inside, causing Mrs. Wolfstein's thighs to feel even swampier than usual.

Finally Manny got up, putting on a bonhomie that looked like a hat on a horse. "Well, folks, it looks like we've made an unscheduled stop."

"How long?" Ms. Weiner tilted the brim of her fedora.

"That depends."

"On what?"

"On how soon I can get this baby fixed." Manny crossed his arms over his chest, more defensively than aggressively. Repairman had never been one of his jobs. The AAA membership for the synagogue might cover the Mitzvah-Mobile, but roadside assistance meant first reaching a phone. No telephone poles, and none of the pine trees seemed to be hooked up. Manny peered uncertainly up ahead. Round the bend was what looked like a pointy-roofed shack, half-hidden by the tree line.

Hope chased fear across Manny's badly shaven face. On the one hand, the building might be inhabited, and that meant the possibility of aid. On the other hand, who the hell knew what crazy bigots lived around here. On the third hand—Manny scratched his head. The women were all looking at him. They had seen the building, too.

"We'll wait for you, dear." Mrs. Wolfstein patted her thighs as if preparing a lap for his return.

"Don't be long." Ms. Weiner dabbed at her brow with a blue bandana she whipped from a side-pocket.

Mrs. Bauman's lipsticked mouth formed the syllable *go*, or maybe it was just Manny's imagination. Mrs. Fishman was gazing at the ceiling of the van.

Manny went. As his Cordovan loafers touched the ground, he felt the sucking embrace of mud. One patch almost swallowed a shoe before he retreated to the blacktop. One foot in front of the other—damn, it was humid—as he made his slow way toward possible salvation. Past the curve, he could see a few beat-up cars and a pickup parked in a semi-circle around the building. Without looking too closely at the sagging structure, he tromped up the three crooked steps and rapped on the door.

A man was speaking inside, but the words were hard to make out. Manny waited ten beats, then knocked louder.

The man's voice plowed on, but the sound of footsteps from the inside approached the door, which was pushed slowly open, almost sweeping him off the steps. A stout black woman wearing the biggest hat Manny had ever seen blocked the doorway. She eyed him up and down. "Whatcha want?"

Manny could make out, through the half-darkness behind her, a few rows of people on plank benches. The black-robed pastor at the back had obviously been delivering a sermon, but he'd stopped, hands in the air, to stare at the intruder. Slowly the other heads turned.

Manny coughed, cleared his throat, and coughed again. "We've had a breakdown." He gestured in the direction of the van down the road.

"A what?" The woman hadn't budged an inch. Her hat, which seemed a cross between a manhole cover and a flower bed, was tilted straight at him.

"The van engine—*kaput*." Manny gave a Bronx cheer to help along the words. "We're down the road about a hundred yards. If

I could just get to a phone, or if anyone here knows something about cars...."

"Hmm. Brother Leroy?" The pastor spoke in a tone rich as an organ, finer than the cantor at the synagogue. The congregation receded from a spot on the third bench, leaving a gap around a gnarled old man in shirt sleeves and a red-checkered tie. The pastor spread his arms as if parting the waters. "See what you can do for the gentleman."

Slowly, as if pulled by cables, Brother Leroy got up and limped toward the entrance. The hat-lady returned to her seat on the last bench to let him by—everything was a close fit inside. Manny looked at the old man doubtfully. "Know much about cars?" he asked.

Brother Leroy pursed his lips. "Some, I reckon. Whuss the problem?"

"It's the engine, I told you. It's just not—cooperating."

Brother Leroy made as if to spit but didn't. "All right, then." He scratched his right arm with his left pinkie. "Less take a look."

As soon as the two were outside the church, the pastor started up again, something about Jesus going an extra mile. A dig at their situation? Manny started walking to the van, but Leroy veered in the direction of the pickup, where he heaved out a massive toolbox, cradling it because the handle was broken off. Leroy headed down the road in a jiggered but rapid gait. "Where you at?" he called back as Manny struggled to catch up.

"Past the bend." Manny pointed. Just beyond the curve, they ran into Ms. Weiner out on her own.

"Wondered what happened to you. Began to worry." She nodded gruffly toward Leroy. "Looks like you got help."

Leroy made a hat-doffing motion without a hat or the use of his hands. When they reached the site of the breakdown, Manny saw Mrs. Fishman and Mrs. Bauman milling in front of the van, Mrs. Fishman glaring at the hood.

Manny performed the introductions. "Ladies, this is Brother Leroy. Brother Leroy, this is Mrs. Fishman"—a vague look from her—"and Mrs. Bauman"—she struck a pose and batted her eyelashes. "Ms. Weiner, you already met"—a tilt of the fedora. "Where's Mrs. Wolfstein?"

"Still in the van." Ms. Weiner shrugged. "Hot in there."

Leroy set the toolbox on a scraggly patch of grass. Then he waited by the roadside in silence for a minute until Manny thought to give him the key.

"Much obliged," said Leroy without a trace of irony and climbed into the van. He settled into the driver's seat, but not before he caught sight of Mrs. Wolfstein stretched across two seats, her rear like twin beach balls. He smacked his lips. "Now *that*," he said to no one in particular, "is a real woman." He turned the key in the ignition, which made a hopeful *chirr-chirr* sound. Then the engine caught with a terrible crunching noise as if it were eating itself. "Not the battery." He leaned out the window towards Manny. "Kinda noise it make before she blew?"

"Sort of a grinding sound." But Manny wanted to sound knowledgeable. "It might've been the distributor cap."

"Not likely." Leroy pulled the hood release and went back outside. When he raised the hood, a dull cloud of steam arose, followed by a scorched odor. "You overheated. Then you drove on it."

"Yeah, yeah." Manny nodded as if he'd known all along. "And so?"

"My guess, the pistons seized up. Might need an engine overhaul."

"No."

"Maybe." Leroy reached into the toolbox and fetched out what looked like an oven mitt. He used it to feel under the hood from an angle Manny couldn't see. "Might could need to rebuild the whole engine if it's bad enough."

"No!"

"Who the mechanic, you or me?" Leroy grinned for the first time, but it wasn't pretty. He stole a glance at Mrs. Wolfstein through the windshield, a frontal view that displayed her heavy bosom. "Tell you what. I'll stay here, try a few things."

"Like what?" This from Ms. Weiner, pacing in a tight line.

"We'll see." But Leroy wasn't really attending to her. He gave a lazy wave in the direction of the lady in the van. Mrs. Wolfstein made an uncertain wave back, her upper arm jiggling. Leroy smacked his lips. Aware that she was somehow cut out of the action, Mrs. Bauman pouted.

Ms. Weiner placed a surprisingly strong hand on Manny's shoulder. "Don't worry. Nothing's gonna happen. But why don't you go back there, see about reinforcements or something?"

Which was how Manny came to be returning to the church with Mrs. Fishman, who'd decided to tag along. "Our van, it's turned into the Mitzvah-Immobile!" she cried. Manny barely cracked a smile as they podged through the mud.

This time, as they neared the building, its function was obvious. In fact, a small rectangular sign by the far side proclaimed, "Turnipseed Baptist Church," and a tinseled spiky cross on the roof drove the point home. Annoyed that he had missed so much, Manny checked his watch: almost noon on a Sunday. In place of the sermon came a loud choral refrain, something about the River Jordan. Mrs. Fishman cocked an ear.

Unwilling to burst in again, Manny waited like a penitent by the door, Mrs. Fishman by his side and peering at the painted planks. The song ended, followed by a short speech and the scraping of benches on a creaking wooden floor. The door opened, once again forcing him off the steps. He and Mrs. Fishman flanked the entrance like greeters as the line of parishioners emerged to stare at them.

A man in a wing-collar and bow tie nodded at them. Twin teenaged girls in starched lavender dresses gazed politely but said nothing. An old man with a cane scrutinized him, frowning. The stout woman in the hat was somewhere in the middle. "Ain'tcha van been fixed yet?"

Manny shrugged. "Working on it."

Mrs. Fishman raised her eyes heavenward with a heartfelt "Gevalt!"

A far bigger woman than the hat lady came out and approached them, carrying a purse the size of a suitcase. She looked them up and down several times. By now they were surrounded. Finally she spoke. "Y'all're Jews, m'I right?"

Manny usually had a few stock answers to this, starting with "What's it to you?" and ending with "Christ was a Jew!" His father would have called out, "*Schwartze!*" But this didn't seem the time or place for such exchanges.

"Jews, eh?" remarked a six-foot bruiser tucked into a shiny black suit. "Where'd they come from?"

"The Red Sea," Manny deadpanned.

"Sure not from round here." Was that the man with the cane?

It was, and he had it raised like a bat. The six-footer flanked him, and on his other side three large women stood like the defensive line-up of the New York Jets. Manny looked around for a way out, as his grandfather might have done during a pogrom.

"Was a Jew killed Christ," muttered one of the women, her purse swinging like a truncheon.

"No, it wasn't either, Ethel," the woman alongside her corrected her. "But it might as well have been."

"Whatcha doin' here, anyway?" The man with the cane swung it as if aiming at a low ball, and spat. "*Northerners.*"

Manny had his back covered only by Mrs. Fishman, who would be a weak reed in this kind of storm. He was about to plead something about live and let live when the pastor's voice rang out from behind the door: "Jews!"

*Oh, shit*, thought Manny, *here it comes.*

"Jews!" the pastor repeated, emerging onto the steps with upraised arms, as if to bless the multitudes. Instead, he touched them both on the heads as if they were singularly promising specimens. "Children of the Book!"

*Thank God for the Old Testament*, thought Manny, falling back against Mrs. Fishman, who held up by leaning into him.

"Brethren," intoned the pastor, "helping these Jews in need

would be a Christian thing to do. I have already dispatched Brother Leroy to assist in repairing their vehicle. Let us now walk to that spot and pray."

"Um, okay." Manny stroked his chin, trying to look scholarly. The congregation stood back to reappraise him, stroking their own chins and nodding.

As the pastor strode off toward the van, the congregation trooped after him like soldiers of the Lord. The day suddenly seemed more vibrant, the sky bluer. The heat was growing almost comfortable. Manny brought up the rear, holding on to Mrs. Fishman's gnarled hand like her sweetheart.

One of the teenagers looked back at them, scratching at her nappy hair. "What're y'all doing in these parts?"

"Doing what comes naturally." This from Mrs. Fishman, whose auditory ability seemed miraculously recuperated, if not her sense of humor.

"Just passing through." That from Manny, still nervous. Were they really going to pray over a set of spark plugs?

When they reached the van, Ms. Weiner was peering balefully under the hood, Mrs. Bauman holding a wrench and a screwdriver like a tool caddy. Brother Leroy was nowhere to be seen—no, there he was in the front seat with Mrs. Wolfstein. When he caught sight of the assemblage through the windshield, he scrambled to get up. "Pastor Jim!" he cried out, half out the door.

The pastor raised a hand as if to confer forgiveness. He moved toward Brother Leroy and began to consult with him in low tones. Manny craned his neck to hear, but all that jumped out was "won't go" and "tried that." At one point, Ms. Weiner barged into the discussion, but added only a shrug. Finally one of the teenage girls was dispatched to the church with some instruction that pulled her shoulders upright. A few minutes passed, during which Ms. Bauman began to talk with the six-foot bruiser, his head bowed to take her in. The stout woman with the manhole hat asked Ms. Weiner where she'd gotten her fedora. Pastor Jim was in the van with Mrs. Wolfstein but soon exited, satisfied that no impropriety had occurred. He bore an odd resemblance to Rabbi Lowenthal, at least around the edges.

When the teenage girl returned, she bore two pitchers on a tray, as in a painting Manny had once seen. He peered into the pitchers and saw water in both of them. Pastor Jim drew the congregation in a half-circle around the front of the van and gazed heavenward. "The Lord is my shepherd," he began. "I shall not want." The congregation chanted along with him like trained sheep. Manny folded his arms in resignation. But when they got to the part about anointing with oil, Pastor Jim rapped one of the jugs with his fingertips and spoke something that could have been Greek—or Aramaic, for all Manny knew. It certainly wasn't Yiddish.

At once, the light around the two pitchers brightened, as if the artist painting the world had erased all shadow. The pastor directed the first pitcher to be poured into the radiator and the second to be poured into the oil tank, with Brother Leroy directing the flow and the flock chanting, "My cup runneth over." The first pitcher poured water, but the second unquestionably yielded oil, thick and dark as honey.

A rousing "Amen" followed. Pastor Jim reached out a hand, into which Brother Leroy placed the key to the van. Raising it to the sky, the pastor blessed it and passed it back to Brother Leroy, who ascended the step with a wave and a grin. A moment later came the miraculous sound of an engine grumbling to life.

Years later, long after Manny had retired from his last job and was living at the Maccabee Assisted Living Home, he still recalled the triumphal roadside procession, the congregation whooping it up, the pastor with his arms upheld, Ms. Weiner throwing her fedora into the air, and Mrs. Wolfstein giving Brother Leroy a big fat kiss. Mrs. Fishman, her hearing restored, now lived down the hall from him, the two sole remaining travelers on that trip, unless you considered all life a journey. The other day, she had opened a Bible and pointed to a verse in Mark, "For he shall make the deaf hear," which for a moment made him suspect her sanity, or maybe even question something greater, but then she laughed, and he realized it was just one of her jokes.

# My Date with Neanderthal Woman

I didn't know whether to bring flowers, which don't say much to someone from a basic subsistence culture. On the other hand, a raw beefsteak might come across as too suggestive, and anyway, I'd read somewhere that Neanderthals were supposed to be vegetarians. So I opted for the middle road, a box of chocolates.

I arrived just as the sun was sinking below the tree line. Glena lived in a cave by the edge of the forest and had, I'd heard, a more natural sense of time than those of us dominated by Rolexes and cell phones. Be that as it may, she wasn't there when I hurt my hand knocking on the cave entrance.

I tried twice, the second time with my foot. Then I called out, emphasizing the glottal *g* I'd heard when her name was pronounced by the TransWorld Dating Agency. She appeared as if suddenly planted in front of me. There she stood, barrel-chested and bandy-legged, not much taller than a stack of tree stumps. Her furry brown hair was matted with sweat, but she smiled at me in a flat-faced way when I held out the chocolate.

Grabbing the box from my hands, she ripped it open and crowed in delight. She stuffed several candies with their wrappers into her mouth and chewed vigorously. The agency had told me not to waste time with complicated verbal behavior, so I just pointed at her and myself and said, "Glena, Robert."

She nodded, then pointed to the chocolate and rubbed her belly. Such a primal response! Frankly, I'd grown tired of modern women and their endless language games. She offered me one of the remaining chocolates from the box, and I was touched: pure reciprocity, though she looked disappointed that I didn't eat the wrappers, as well. When she began to polish off the box itself, I shook my head, smiling. I mimed eating and pointed away from the forest. I would take her out to dinner. Neanderthals, I recalled, were often on the cusp of starvation. At any rate, she seemed to understand and followed me obediently as I led her to Chez Asperge, a small French-fusion-vegan restaurant not too far from the woods.

Chez Asperge is elegant but casual, and we were greeted heartily by Claude, the maitre d'. I may have misinterpreted those raised Gallic eyebrows. I didn't know that the place had a dress code. In fact, the little loincloth Glena wore made me feel overdressed. Anyway, the situation was fixed with a borrowed jacket, which Glena chose to wear in a charmingly asymmetric fashion.

God, I hate all the introductory explanations of a first date—which is why I was so happy none of that mattered to Glena. With an easy familiarity as if she'd known me for years, she spread her arms on the table and scooped up half the mashed lentil dip. It's true: a woman who enjoys her food is sexy. She offered me some, and I showed her how to spread it on pita. But knives seemed to frighten her, and I'm sorry about that scar on the table. Still, we had a lovely meal—she particularly enjoyed the raw vegetable plate.

After dinner, I walked her home along the forest path. Movies and clubs could come later, if at all. I didn't want to overstimulate her. Even electric lights made her twitch a bit. But along the path, the moon was out, illuminating Glena's short but powerful body in a way that was weirdly beautiful. When I reached for her hand, at first she jerked back—different cultures have different intimacy rites, the agency guy said—so I took pains to explain that my intentions were honorable. Maybe she couldn't understand the words, yet I think she got the gist. And anyway, there's a limit to what I can achieve by gestures.

Eventually, her hand crept around mine and nearly crushed it. My miming of pain, hopping on one foot and flailing, made her laugh. A sense of humor is very important in a relationship.

We paused at the entrance to her cave. She smiled, the gaps in her teeth drawing me in. Her earthy aroma was vaguely aphrodisiac. What came next was sort of a kiss, followed by a rib-cracking embrace that the osteopath says is healing nicely. Soon after, she retreated to her cave. Still, whenever I think about it, I feel twinges. What a woman! I'd like to invite her out this weekend, but I can't e-mail her. Maybe I'll just drop by her cave accidentally on purpose with a bouquet of broccoli.

Yes, yes, I know all the objections. Some couples are separated by decades, but we're separated by millennia. I like rock music and she likes the music of rocks. I'm modern Cro-Magnon and she's Neanderthal, but I think we can work out our differences if we try.

# Afternoon of a Poet

Vinnie Cartolucci could locate the exact moment he became a poet. He was working in Loading at Emerson Electric, going back to the hangar for another load of AC units, when he noticed that the steel boxes looked like coffins. He blinked. The light seemed to grow simultaneously darker and lighter as the impact of the image came home to him. The linkage between industrialization and death was symbolized by the gunmetal surfaces, so mute and gray. Yet the AC units were going to be loaded onto a truck, to be purchased by consumers all over the country and reborn into their homes. He paused to wipe the sweat off his brow with a dirty blue bandana.

The paradox inherent in the death and birth imagery puzzled him. But as he drove the forklift under a five-container stack, a line entered his mind: "The green-gray circuit where life is rearranged." That wasn't quite right—something off in the syntax—so he fiddled with it for a while. It seemed to go with another line that developed in his mind as mysteriously as the first had appeared, along with a tough logic that held both together, something about the pregnant hulls of warships.

A few minutes later, he walked up to Mort the foreman, who was supervising another shipment. "Hey," he said, tapping Mort on the arm, "I need to borrow your pen."

Driving home that evening, Vinnie barely felt the three beers he'd knocked back at Hoofer's. He was preoccupied with the color gray and the word *fustian*, which he wanted to look up as soon as he got to a library. He owned no dictionary, and his live-in girl-friend Celia didn't care much for books, though she did have an amazing CD collection spanning ABBA to Ziggie Stardust.

"You look sorta out of it," remarked Celia when Vinnie began frowning at the take-out pizza.

"Pizza, *pizza*...ever struck you what a weird sound that is?"

"Yeah, well, nothing beats a pizza." Celia slapped her thigh. "Hey, that rhymes!"

Vinnie rubbed his eyes. For the first time, he recognized that he was living with a linguistically challenged individual. Later that night, when he couldn't sleep, he began keeping a journal. "Words don't make it happen but they change what they describe," he wrote in sloppy script. "The limit of my words are the sky of my world." He also jotted down the first line of a villanelle, only to realize that he wasn't a formalist and in fact had no idea of how the lines went after the opening tercet. After he finished it, he tossed it into a folder magic-markered "JUVENILIA." He began dressing in black and walking around with an *Oxford Book of English Verse*. Half the time, he had no idea what the lines meant—"With pungent sauces, multiply variety / In a wilderness of mirrors"?—but that only inflamed his passion. In a week, he had come out from under the influence of Eliot and was wondering how the hell Larkin did it.

On the job, he was bemused. The whole loading area had taken on an air of gray-green melancholy, tinged by urine sniffs and metallic clangs (he was experimenting with synesthesia). Lunch hour he spent thinking of analogies for his current employment: a second grade classroom, the moment before sunrise, an ant crawling on a rotten log. Tony from the motor division wanted to know what the hell he was writing, but Vinnie just shrugged. Being a poet, he was beginning to understand, meant being misunderstood a lot.

Celia didn't really appreciate his birthday lyric to her, which began, "Celia, the light from my cigarette butt."

"Especially that part about 'ashy splendor'—what the hell's that supposed to mean?" Celia, in a wife-beater and cutoffs, looked both provocative and provoked, a phrase he stole for his journal.

"It's just a metaphor." He sighed and took back the poem. "Look, if you want a Hallmark greeting card—"

"That's what you gave me last year."

"Sure, but I wasn't—." He paused. Wasn't what? A poet then? The word still sounded strange on his lips. "I wasn't serious," he finally said, insulting Celia for the rest of the day. When he tried to explain further, he hurt her for the rest of the week. To console himself, he sent out three batches of poems he had completed since his strange metamorphosis. One set received an immediate rejection, the second somehow disappeared, and the third was accepted by an obscure quarterly that promised publication within the next two years.

Meanwhile, work was becoming intolerable. He couldn't concentrate on driving the forklift when *utility* rhymed with *futility*. Then the guys stole his notebook and read sections from it at lunch in lisping pansy voices. At home, Celia became moody and withdrawn. When Vinnie found a newspaper in the bathroom with a few personal ads circled, he also found a poignant poetry in some of the wording and made notes for a long narrative poem based on it.

He lost his job at the Emerson plant.

His style became more obscure.

Celia moved out on Thursday, leaving a misspelled note.

When he hit rock bottom, he scribbled "the cliché of despair" in his notebook and wandered around putting down lit cigarettes in odd places. But time marched on like an unfinished simile. Just as he was about to settle into a life of alienation, he woke up one morning to find that all poetic urges and talent had left him. *Maxim* looked good to him again, *American Poetry Review* unreadable. And what was this horseshit he'd written about gray-green commercial depths? He threw out his notebook. Celia came back after a week, and they celebrated with a beer-bust. He snagged a job at the municipal waste disposal plant, remarkably similar to his old work.

These days he seems reasonably content, except for an odd moment or two every day when he stares at the flapping edges of a disused carton, or sniffs the incinerator smoke and thinks of a gull in mid-flight, a dense haze descending like the paw of God.

# Crusade

Pedaling into the wind, Henry downshifted to a 39-17 for the upcoming hill. The redneck tyke on the trike crossed his path a moment later.

The incline was a six-percent grade five miles past the county line of Blanton, where the loblolly pines along the roadside suddenly thickened as if massing for a confrontation. CR 221 was an indifferently slagged road with unpredictable dips and turns as it ran past kudzu valleys and the occasional trailer. The folks who lived there razzed Henry, and he'd had dirt clods flung at his back. Lately it had gotten worse. On his old Colnago racing bike, hunched over the bars in his Lycra shorts and jersey, he was clearly a geek they had to poke fun at. He'd changed routes twice, but rednecks lived in trailers near Booneville and Monroe, too. Besides, this was the only training hill around.

The kid on the trike came from nowhere, as if he'd scooted out between two trees, and then he was in front of Henry's wheel. Henry squeezed the brakes hard and found himself skidding out. His right thigh and arm slid along the pressed-in gravel. The horizon spun. His cleat was stuck in the quick-release pedal, the Colnago on top of him like a giant lovesick crab.

When he looked up, he could see the kid still slowly pedaling his tricycle a few yards away. It was one of those Big Wheel specials with a spiral design on the front wheel that radiated inward as it turned, towards some idiotic zero. The kid was far too big for the trike, as if he'd been held back in school for a few years and was in the wrong grade. He was dressed in a dirty T-shirt and overalls, his knees and elbows jutting outward.

"Hey, why don't you watch where you're going!" Henry felt the sting of road rash and knew he'd be prickly sore tomorrow. He picked himself up gingerly, looking at his bike to see if it was still rideable. The saddle sat an off-angle and the handlebar tape was torn. Only then did he examine the extent of his own damage, redness oozing from the skinned areas.

The kid had stopped pedaling and looked back to watch as Henry checked the drive train and the wheels. The front wheel was out of true, rubbing against the brake pads. He took out his spoke wrench from the kit underneath his saddle and set to work.

"Well, aren't you going to say anything?" he shouted to the kid, who by now, like the chicken in the joke, had crossed to the other side. "You could've gotten killed!"

The kid gave him the finger and disappeared into the far trees. Henry was about to yell something else and thought of hobbling after him in his cycling shoes, but then he figured what the hell. Besides, he sensed somehow that he was being watched. As he pedaled painfully away, the trees on the far left parted, and Henry thought he saw the blue-black gleam of a shotgun barrel.

Back home, ten miles east in Lyon, he gingerly cleaned his wounds with hydrogen peroxide, which stung like a carpet of wet needles. He lived in a cracker-box apartment a mile away from Lyon Ag Junior College, the school where he taught English. He was thirty-one years old and grudgingly celibate, having broken up with his girlfriend in New Jersey when he'd taken this job after grad school.

"Hen," Charlotte had told him as he was filling the U-Haul for the trip down south, "since you're packing anyway, maybe we should just pack it in." She was addicted to puns as a way of connecting. She also knew how he hated to be called Hen or Harry. In addition, she told him she was seeing someone else, had been since January. So Henry had driven over a thousand miles in a rented van filled with old possessions and new rage, which had slowly settled into directed sullenness his first few weeks in Lyon (pronounced "Line" by its residents). Bicycling, which had been his sport in college, had brought him back to himself. He'd gradually extended his rides range to a thirty-mile range around Blanton County.

Limping to the kitchen, his bandages so badly applied that they hung like crepe paper, he pulled some gray roast beef, a spongy loaf of bread, and an orange from the fridge and fed himself some lunch. He spent the rest of that afternoon, which happened to be a Saturday, correcting papers and preparing for next week's classes. In his lit survey, they were reading O'Connor's "A Good Man Is Hard to Find." As the red eye of the sun slid bloodily below the tree line and the crickets began their evening racket, he made a strong notation next to the line "It's no real pleasure in life." The accident kept replaying in his mind.

The next day, stiff and swollen, he went out on his bike anyway, the pain subsiding a bit after a few miles. His new cycling shorts had ripped obscenely in the crash, and he couldn't find his old pair just then, so he made do with some swimming trunks he'd scared up from one of his moving boxes, which doubled as a clothing drawer. He defiantly rode the same route around the same time as the day before. He wasn't going to let some punk on a tricycle put him off, though he kept a watch tight as a shifter cable on the pavement ahead of him.

But he met no one. It was only by the time he passed the town of Stokes and its Beacon of Light church, an off-white warehouse with a parking lot full of pickups and Ed Dorados, that he realized where all of them were. Henry raced by the building with the contempt of a hardened nonbeliever.

Monday, he went over the O'Connor story in class, only to have a heavyset young woman ask why the author was making fun of crackers.

Henry tried a different avenue. "I think she's making fun of everyone." The class frowned.

"Not nice to make fun of people," observed a rangy guy in front who actually took notes. "Didn't you say she died young?"

"Yes, but that wasn't what did her in." Henry let his gaze settle on the only attractive woman in the class, a sweater girl named Nancy. "Anyway, what killed the family in the story?"

"Bein' a busybody," volunteered the heavyset woman.

*

Tuesday afternoon, Henry had a near-accident with a Ford pick-up. He was halfway through a bend around a cornfield when the truck zoomed in front of him, then decelerated. This time he was able to swerve, missing the rear bumper by a foot or so. Probably drunk, he thought, and put his head down to power away. In half a minute, he'd left the pickup behind.

But the noise of an engine caught up with him around the next bend. The pickup was following along, weaving loosely in his path. He clicked into the big ring and had started motoring at over 25 m.p.h. when the *brap* of a honk almost lifted him out of his seat. He looked back reflexively. The pickup was just a wheel-length behind, the driver grinning crookedly behind the cracked windshield. He wore a mullet that jounced with the truck.

Henry shook his head and edged toward the shoulder. He motioned for the pickup to come around.

The pickup veered to the shoulder and came after him. The grill had almost kissed his wheel when Henry found a burst of speed and cut over to the left hand side of the road. The pickup slowed down for a moment like a puzzled beast, then zagged after him.

"Make up your mind!" Henry shouted as if he were communicating with someone he could talk to. "Pass or drop back!"

The pickup driver leaned out the window, one arm drooped around the window. "Do *what* now?" He reached below the dashboard to hoist a beer can.

Henry swerved to the shoulder again and narrowly missed wiping out on some gravel. "CYCLIST FOUND IN DITCH," he could see tomorrow's headline in *The Lyon Letter*. "Lyon Ag Mourns Loss." But just as he was wondering whether to ditch the bike and try his luck on foot, a big green S.U.V. came humming from the other direction. It slowed a bit as it neared the cyclist and truck, and that might've scared the driver pursuing him—because the pickup roared off, pinging gravel and dirt, the empty beer can tossed out the window.

Henry slowed to a crawl and caught his breath. That was just too damned close. But when he stopped by the local police station, the cop up front was less than helpful.

"Can't go on much with just a description of the vehicle." The policeman slowly but firmly shook his head as if closing a door with it. "Anyway, if we do bring him in, it's your word against his." He took another look at Henry, still in his biking gear plus a few bandages. "Maybe you should take up some other sport."

The next day, Henry was in what passed for a faculty lounge, a few ratty chairs and a coffee machine in a spare room. He was complaining to the one friend he'd made in the three months he'd been here, Tom Watkins in sociology. "I'm telling you, it's not like I did anything to them. I just ride my bike."

"In a clown suit. With a sign that reads, 'I'm not from around here.'" Tom took a pull on his stained "Genius at Work" coffee mug. He taught a course called Social Deviancy, which the students had nicknamed Nuts 'n' Sluts. "What do you expect?"

"Some consideration, that's what!" Henry sloshed down his mug on the nearby foldout bridge table so it made a double ring on the surface. "What the hell are they thinking? That's what I'd like to know."

"Maybe if they thought you shared some of their values."

"Don't give me that sociology-speak. I'm never going to be like them."

Tom sipped and grinned. "So? Fake it."

That afternoon, Henry was teaching Nathaniel Hawthorne's "Young Goodman Brown" from the fat anthology when a guy with a trucker's cap in the middle row raised his hand. "That guy really the devil in the forest?"

Henry waved his hand grandly. Never answer a question that you can get your students to answer. "What do *you* think?"

A woman wearing a WWJD T-shirt spoke up. "Our preacher told us to watch out for people like him. You can go to hell for less."

"You don't think Goodman Brown—look at his name—is on some kind of quest?"

"Mm...maybe." The woman screwed up her face as if Henry's query were a gnat buzzing about her chin. "That'd make it different."

"You mean doin' it for the glory of God." The trucker's-cap guy scratched his head through the headband. "I reckon."

If Henry had been a cartoon character, a light bulb would have lit up over his head. But in fact nothing much happened except a warped discussion of the story that petered out after a few more comments. Henry moved on to the subject of allegory, which interested only a few members of the class, and that was it.

That night, though, after washing up the dishes from a semi-successful tuna casserole, he had an idea. He got in his battered Honda to make a shopping run.

Thursday at 4:23, Henry was barreling toward his hill when he saw a familiar-looking pickup coming the other way, cracked windshield and all. Shit, he thought, this is when it happens.

The mullet-head at the wheel reached for something on the seat beside him. A beer can? A rock?

Henry smiled and waved. He sat up in the saddle.

The redneck slowed down to squint at Henry's helmet and jersey. There, in golden letters, big and small, Henry had glue-gunned "BIKIN FOR JESUS." He widened his smile till it hurt.

The pickup slowed even more as the guy leaned out the window. He gave a thumbs-up. "Amen to that, bro!"

Henry nodded, then put his head down again. He jammed up the hill in his big ring and coasted down the long, slanting other side in exultation.

The next day, he received salutes from a spade-bearded man and his wife, the lone spectators of his ride, who looked as if they had been planted by the side of the road. Over the course of the next week, he got waves and jolly honks from a whole slew of folks, even an aging Hell's Angel type on a Harley Davidson.

"I fixed the problem we were talking about," he told Tom without elaborating as he passed him in the hallway.

"What'd you do, buy a chopper?"

"Let's just say I'm riding high." And he went on to teach "My heart leaps up when I behold" in his lit survey. The class appreciated the cheap sentiment, especially the line about natural piety, and for once he didn't disabuse them. That afternoon, he time-trialed five one-mile circuits that took in three cotton fields, a saw-toothed kudzu gulch, and the white clapboard Beacon of Light (MB, Deacon Floyd), where a woman emerged from the front steps just as he was gunning down the straightaway. Ordinarily, he would've stomped on the pedals and not looked back, but he'd become increasingly conscious of his message. The woman carried a platter and a pitcher, transferring both to the crook of her left arm in order to wave. She was both lithe and bosomy, like an Arabian dream of an houri, and Henry gave her his best smile even as he tried not to grit his teeth against the ache in his quads. On the fifth circuit, she was still there, so he doubled back after the finish, braking at her feet.

"You sure do ride fast." Her smile was pearlescent, her hips like a lyre.

"I'm on a crusade." The words were out of his mouth before he knew it.

"For Jesus, huh."

"I guess you could say that."

She touched his helmet gingerly. "Not many guys around here like you."

"I, um, teach at the college."

"Really?" That smile again. Henry imagined what it must be like to encircle that slim waist, to enter that pretty red cave of a mouth. "Well, maybe I should enroll."

It was a while before Henry got moving again, and it wasn't his quads that ached but something more central. Back in his apartment, he took the edge off with a stingingly cold shower.

Two days later, at the foot of the hill, the trike tyke tried to ride with him. Henry paced him for a hundred yards or so, nodding in encouragement, then took off. The tyke was replaced the next afternoon by a little girl, who offered him a basket of cookies. She said her mama had baked them. When a teenager with a stick tried to thrust it through Henry's spokes, he jerked it back as if burnt when he saw Henry's yellow Jesus jersey. A girl Henry knew in the art department had silk-screened an image of the Savior, staring out from Henry's back and chest.

The lone reporter from *The Lyon Letter*, Jim Carruthers, came to interview Henry at his office. He wore retro suspenders and a pork pie hat. "They're calling you the cycling crusader in the valley," he told Henry, settling in the fold-out chair offered to him. "Had a vision or something?"

Henry thought of the woman by the church, whom he'd come across three more times, whose name was Tammy, and whom he'd arranged to see this Friday evening. "Several," he said.

"Are you affiliated with a particular church?"

Henry had to think about that one. "The First Church of Christcycle," he finally came up with. And that was what the *Letter* put in its Friday edition.

"'Christcycle'—that's a good one." Tom slapped the newspaper, which featured a photo of Henry on his Colnago, looking somehow both saintly and competitive. The two of them were in the faculty lounge, waiting for the coffee machine to finish its muddy business. "Did you mean it when you said—wait, let me find that part—'every revolution of the spokes brings me closer to God'?"

"I had to tell him *something*." Henry stared away from his likeness. "I never realized how religious people were around here until this started."

"The pressure to conform, maybe. Freud called it mass psychosis." Tom stroked his mug absently as if it were a small pet. "*I* say you've opened a can of worms."

On CR 225, Henry rode past a Y junction that bore a sheet banner, "WELCOME FIRST CHURCH OF CHRISTCYCLE RIDERS." Henry noted the plural and wondered what was up. During the final leg back into town, just past a four-way stop, he was joined by a teenage girl on a Schwinn and a couple on an old tandem. They bore their own "BIKIN FOR JESUS" credo on their shirts and told him howdy. Henry thought briefly of blowing them off his back wheel but recalled his newly exalted status and instead grandly led the procession back into town.

That evening, he escorted Tammy to Storell's Fish Shack, which had the best hushpuppies in the county. Henry had made an effort with a sports jacket his father had once owned, but Tammy wore a tank top that showed off an impressive set of pecs. They talked about the glory of exercise, and Henry murmured, "*Mens sana in corporo sano.*"

Tammy, it turned out, was an inline skater and had the calves to prove it. But she belittled her activity. "Somehow 'skatin' for Christ' doesn't have the same ring."

"I don't know about that," said Henry gallantly. He was feeling pretty magnanimous, not to mention horny. Then again, he thought, good Christians don't get promiscuous.

He was wrong there. Tammy was recently divorced, she let drop, and in the mood for a laying-on of hands. At the doorstep of her apartment on the edge of town, she leaned into his embrace and

delivered a soul kiss that was absolutely breathtaking. He stag-
gered home with visions of heavenly bliss circling his anatomy.

The following Monday, he was called into the dean's office.
Dean Kutz, who fancied himself a dandy, fingered his amethyst tie
clip. "I see you've got some press in the *Letter*."

"Some." Henry scratched his chin. "You know how the press
distorts things."

Dean Kutz looked up at an angle as if he'd been slapped. "You
mean it's not true?"

"I wouldn't say that. It's just not exactly—." But he stopped
there, transfixed by the look the dean was giving him. "Let's just
say I'm no saint."

Kutz reached out to clap him on the shoulder. "Amen to that.
We all struggle."

Henry left the dean's office, wondering whether the act had
gone far enough. But when his afternoon class on Shelley's "To a
Sky-Lark" came across as more preaching than teaching, he all but
got a standing ovation. A punkoid no name with a scowl etched
onto his features suddenly looked penitent, and the nubile Nancy
sat there in the second row with her lips parted in a perfect O, as
if ready to kiss the rod. Roosevelt's phrase "a bully pulpit" never
sounded so apt. Stuffed into his faculty mailbox was a homemade
orange loaf-cake and a note from one of the secretaries. He went
out to ride that afternoon feeling lordly.

He rode his afternoon miles with a dozen disciples, ranging
from training wheels to tandem, stomping ahead and looping back
whenever he felt the need to extend himself. When they encountered a drunk driving an El Camino, Henry led the pack in a hymn
as they forced the car onto the shoulder. One of the riders on the
tandem used her cell phone to call the police, who arrived five
minutes later and issued a DUI. It was the same cop who'd told
Henry to take up another sport.

Jim Carruthers wrote a front-pager about the incident. The story
was picked up by AP and published in the regional *Star Clarion* the

next day. "CHURCH OF CHRISTCYCLE RULES THE ROAD," read the headline. Someone clipped the article and taped it above the departmental copier. That Wednesday, he was called by a publicist named who offered to manage his image. And that evening Tammy took him to heaven in her futon bed. "Jesus," he breathed as she mounted him and began to pump. He felt as if someone were watching over him. But he also felt as if someone might be peeping in the slanted window, and when he got up to enter the cramped bathroom, he heard footsteps outside and an engine starting up. By the time he pulled on his pants and checked around, whoever it was had gone.

He came back into the bedroom, his feeling of invulnerability slackened. "You got any nosy friends? I thought I heard someone out there."

"Just a jealous ex." Tammy sat up and looked through the window. "But he knows I'll slap a restraining order on him if he tries anything." At which point his angel spread her pectorals and drew him in again. Still, she looked a bit troubled.

That night he dreamed of demons on three-speeds, led by an imp on a tricycle. The dawn came tranquil and cloudless, but Tammy had to leave early for work at the Emerson plant. He dressed clumsily and walked home, feeling unprotected without his helmet and jersey. Shoved under his office door at school was a crabbed note written in Magic Marker, bearing three words: "*Watch your ass.*" A betrayal by one of his disciples? Were people looking at him differently? For his afternoon literature class, he taught an excerpt from Tennyson's *In Memoriam* and left to ride.

Someone had slashed his front clincher, which he could have taken as a sign. Instead, he pulled off the ruined tire, hunted around for a new 23cc from last month's bike-catalogue mail order, and stretched the bead over the rim. But it took a while, and by the time he reached the start-off point for his ride, only three disciples were still around: the tandem couple and the teenage girl on her Schwinn.

Yesterday's annoyance was today's disappointment. "Where'd everyone go?"

The girl, who had something wrong with her lip, jerked her thumb up the road. "They went ahead."

"We'll catch them." Henry instructed his three followers to stay on his back wheel and slowly accelerated along CR 204. Scraggly pines stood like sentinels flanking the road. The sky was the azure of infinity and completely cloudless, a preternatural calm in the March air. As predicted, they soon caught up with the rest of the flock, but Henry kept up his punishing pace and soon outdistanced them all. A few minutes later, he was out of sight. Cycling these days made him feel as if he floating an inch off the pavement. For the first time in his life, he had prestige, and it colored his vision. At times he even felt vaguely holy, as if he were on a mission. He bore hard on the pedals, head down, his helmet bearing his message to the world.

The Dodge Ram came out of nowhere. One moment, Henry was alone on the road, and the next he was being paced by the chunky pickup. He had no time to swerve or even cry out. The truck ran him right into the roadside ditch and stopped a few yards ahead. "Teach you to mess around with Tammy!" yelled the driver, glaring back.

Henry couldn't reply. He had fallen badly, twisting his shoulder. Before he could even move, a bearish man got out of the Dodge and stumped his way toward him. Taking rough aim, he kicked Henry once in the ribs and twice in the head.

The pain that shot through Henry's spine was like a spark flaring and then being extinguished. Forced to look up at the sun, Henry saw the light filtering through the trees, haloing the man's beard as he got back in the Dodge and drove away. The Colnago lay to the side of him, its front wheel pretzeled. His flimsy helmet was split in two. A line about the wages of sin flitted through his damaged brain. His gaze fixed just above the horizon, he saw his flock pedaling inexorably toward him, two hundred yards, then one hundred yards away, like medieval knights on curious mounts. The afternoon sun seemed to bathe them all in blood. But then from the woods, at an angle Henry could barely spy, came another rider, not the tyke on the trike, but a bent-over figure on a black bicycle. The rider wore no helmet but instead a cowl, and strapped to his thigh was a scythe.

# An Academic Proposition

On April 23rd, Shakespeare's alleged birthday, Professor Henry Twistle mentioned that he'd guarantee an *A* to any student who'd favor him with a blow job. He let his gaze linger particularly over Mary Bucek's big lips, as well as on Joey Ginelli's perfect, sullen Cupid's bow. But the professor let off his small bombshell just as class was letting out, and amid the stuffing of book bags and scraping of chairs, few students could be sure they'd heard what they had. Professor Twistle himself was looking elsewhere, and no one was inclined to ask him to repeat the statement.

Afterwards, in the comparative privacy of the women's locker room, Mary asked her friend Tanya whether Twistle could've possibly said it.

"Oh, I don't know," answered Tanya as she removed her lacy teal bra to put on her black elastic sports bra. Both women were on the women's soccer team. "These days, who can tell? My sister at State says she knows a prof who sniffs all the blue-books. And she could swear there was cum on hers when he handed it back to her."

They both laughed. Five minutes later, they hit the field running.

But Joey told Harvey Lamport, who told two of his football jock friends, one of whom scrawled a graffiti message about it in the men's room at the library. Eventually, the news attracted the ear of the head of liberal arts, a deanish man named Michael

Mallon. Exquisitely mindful of suits and counter-suits, he prepared himself for a ticklish phone call.

"Hank? Mike. Fine, fine...right." He paused and took a breath. "Listen, the janitor who cleans the library bathrooms says he saw something written about you and an act of fellatio...."

"Oh, *that*. Sex for an *A*." Twistle chuckled. "Don't worry, I don't think anyone'll take me up on it."

"But—let me get this straight—you *did* make the offer?"

"Well, yes. You know, after fifteen years of teaching, by God, I think I'm entitled to more than forty exams at the end of the term."

"Y...es. I can see your point...." eased Mallon, who'd wondered that himself when he was still teaching in the history department. "Only, Hank, don't you think this might have...unfavorable repercussions?"

Twistle sounded genuinely surprised. "Why? I'm not offering anything I can't deliver on. You know, students nowadays are so cynical, I thought this might actually restore a little faith in the system. *Quid pro quo*, I mean."

"Um." Mallon thought about what to say, thought better of it, and finally said, "Okay. But for God's sake, don't act on what you said. My guess is that the students probably didn't take you seriously. I mean, no one's filed a harassment charge. Yet. Anyway, thanks for clearing this up."

But not all students are cynical. Some are earnest. Twistle's first offer came from Ellen Sparks, whose shapely shorts he had admired when teaching Plato's *Symposium* at the beginning of the term. When she knocked on his office door, he was masturbating over "The Reeve's Tale" in Chaucer, but he quickly zipped himself up.

"Come in, come in," he announced airily.

Ellen dutifully entered, bearing her latest essay, marked with a red *C*. After discussing its shortcomings, she turned to look directly at him. "Did you really mean what you said that day, about a blow job for an *A*?"

Twistle smiled vaguely, reminiscently, disarmingly, lewdly. He nodded almost imperceptibly.

Within a minute, Ellen had kneeled in front of him and was addressing his fly. Her hands were soft but practiced. The carmine depth of her mouth was like wet velvet. As she bent to her task, Twistle let his hands stray to her full buttocks. Before she left, he had crossed out the offending *C* and changed it to an *A* with a "Sorry, my mistake."

News got around. Next came Marjorie Buckler, a cheerleader who couldn't understand poetry to save her soul. "Take it slowly. Don't choke," Twistle gently advised when she bore down a bit too enthusiastically.

Among the volunteers was also one guy, Albert Saxe, who acted nervous the whole time, despite Twistle's assurances that he would treat him the same as the women. The incident did add to Twistle's growing reputation for non-sexism, as well as re-answering that familiar, exasperated question, "Just what do I have to do around here to get an A, anyway?"

No one complained, the class actually seemed to go better than before, and the greater ease in marking papers made Twistle much happier. No one except a sadist likes to give bad grades. When Mallon called near the end of the semester to inquire how things were going, Twistle said, "Wonderful."

That spring, enrollment in Twistle's literature humanities class was slightly up from last semester. Some of the students seemed almost overly attentive, as if waiting for certain words to drop from the head of the class.

But Twistle had grown jaded and didn't make the offer this time.

# What the Thunder Said

For fifteen years, or a total of forty-five semesters including the summer sessions, Professor Eric Slough had taught at Wonomac College. And each semester, Professor Slough had put *The Waste Land* on his syllabus, first as part of the British literature survey but gradually paring down all other material until T. S. Eliot's *chef d'oeuvre*, as Slough repeatedly referred to it, was the centerpiece of each course. After he received tenure, largely on the strength of his publications on Eliot's stunted sublimity in the poem, it was often the only item on his syllabi, much to the consternation of students and administrators.

This monopoly occurred not only in his upper-level British Modernism seminar but also in his British literary surveys, his Introlit class, and even in the one annual composition section he was forced to teach. "Eliot's technique of composition," he remarked to his department chair, a large and rumpled but reticent man named McGowan, "combined with Pound's editing prowess are invaluable training for first-year writing students." He fingered his tie, a sort of paisley design that had grown unfocused over the years. "Look at 'The Fire Sermon.' If that isn't a perfect specimen of an edited text, I don't know what is."

"But," began McGowan, but "but" was usually as far as he got.

"Fine," replied Slough and shuffled off, the large folio edition of *The Waste Land* facsimile and transcript tucked under his arm like a kickboard.

Students who took one of Professor Slough's courses were invariably impressed with his knowledge of the poem's sources, though generally depressed that they would be spending an entire semester examining one poem. "I mean, there's gotta be more to Brit lit than *this*," complained Daniel Fogarty, who'd gotten annoyed at all the German in "The Burial of the Dead."

"*The Waste Land*, Eliot's *chef d'oeuvre*, contains all of Brit lit, as you call it," intoned Slough loftily. "Now, if you'll just look at the stanza that begins, 'Unreal City,' we can start to piece out some of the allusions to Baudelaire and the French tradition, as well."

Professor Slough was slyer than most administrators gave him credit for, however. When feminist forces massed on the horizon, he promptly offered a seminar entitled "Women in *The Waste Land*," and when multiculturalism stole feminism's fire, he offered the poem as a panoply of utterances from all over the world. "Eliot was originally going to call his *chef d'oeuvre* 'He do the police in different voices,'" he pointed out, dwelling particularly long on the Sanskrit repetition at the end.

Slough's battered copy of the poem, a miracle of rare device, was heavily annotated and somehow spliced to sheets of legal paper, the whole thing stuffed into a folder stamped *TSE* on the cover in fading violet ink. Armed with his folder, Slough could lecture, sometimes engagingly, on subjects as diverse as Tarot cards—"I have a pack right here," he would announce, drawing the deck from his breast pocket and executing a shuffle of Vegas complexity—and scatology—"The whole scene with the clerk and the typist is an unfinished, sordid double sonnet. Now what words rhyme with 'kiss' and 'unlit'?"

But in his sixteenth year at Wonomac, opposition began to mount against his *Waste Land*-only policy. For one thing, McGowan took early retirement and was replaced by a harder headed chair named Ellen Sanders. "Look," she told him at the start of the fall semester, "I have the greatest respect for T. S. Eliot, but you can't just teach him exclusively."

"A great work of literature," Slough proclaimed, "contains infinite depth and may be reread continually."

"Maybe so, but what about students who want to take you for more than one course?" Professor Sanders leaned back uncomfortably in her departmental chair, whose back conformed more to McGowan's contours than hers.

"What *about* them?" Slough adjusted his tie, another paisley design that looked like his others but from a different angle. "Many students have profitably retaken my classes." This was true: the more the students knew the poem, the better they did in Slough's classes. Doing Slough twice, as more and more students were discovering, was a bit of a snooze, but also an easy *A*.

"All right, but the administration doesn't like it."

Slough smiled grimly. *Da*: give, sympathize, control. "I've heard you talk about just what the dean can do with his comments."

"Yes, well. Your contract states..." But here Professor Sanders could go no further because in fact the terms of his employment stated nothing at all about the content of his courses. So she let him go with a toothless warning.

In the end, a twitchy student named Marlene Price seized the initiative. Having taken Slough the second time around to boost her average, she found herself unable to bear the lessons of "A Game of Chess" once again. An hour before Tuesday's class, she snuck into Professor Slough's office, stole his *TSE* folder, and drove a mile away off campus to drop it into a dumpster. *That oughta put you in rat's alley*, she thought, hugging herself lightly.

Professor Slough was five minutes late for class that day. His head was wagging, and his hands clenched at little nothings in the air. "Class," he announced, pausing to rest his hands on the rostrum, "*someone* has walked off with my Eliot folder."

An excited hush fell over the class. Marlene, seated in the back row next to a basketball player named Stan Rogers, had to bite her lip to stop from cackling. What would happen next? What would go on for the rest of the term? Professor Slough looked as if he could connect nothing with nothing, and for a moment Marlene actually felt sorry for him. She wondered what the collection time for the dumpster was, and whether it was already too late. She focused on Slough's open lips as they slowly pressed together into a little purse.

"Luckily for all of us," he continued, "I've memorized all my notes. So if you open your poem to page seven, the lines that begin, 'My nerves are bad to-night,' I think we can safely proceed. Notice how Eliot, who famously remarked that poetry is an escape from personality, has slyly worked his marriage into this exchange." Professor Slough leaned over the rostrum and fastened upon Marlene. "Ms. Price, can you tell us what's going on here?"

# Hiatus

There are limits to everything, from pedagogy to patience. One Thursday morning, teaching in the fluorescent gloom of Lowen Hall, Professor Irene Cantwell decided she'd had enough. The revelation came to her in the middle of a sentence about Emerson, stopping her in mid sentence as she was chalking "transcendentalism" on the blackboard. She looked closely at what she had written, with the astigmatic stare of the professional academic, then turned to face her students. The array of faces, notebooks, and poised pens neither consoled her nor depressed her. She simply knew it was time to leave, so she did—walking unhurriedly out of room 404A, exiting Lowen Hall, and proceeding to her Honda Civic three blocks away in the faculty parking lot.

Only after she'd driven two miles did the force of what she'd done hit home. She had nothing with her—no papers, no books. She hadn't even bothered to stop at her office, that repository of critical texts piled on top of chairs, where her bookshelf had conceded defeat, with an old manual typewriter perched by the window sill like a metal bird grown too heavy for flight.

"My God, you've done it now." "You go, girl!" "What about my career?" These were all possible responses, yet none of this flitted through her mind. Rather than smite her forehead or slam on the brakes, she merely accelerated through the yellow light at Hanford Boulevard, and in another five minutes she was home.

In the cozy but book-clogged warren of her apartment, Professor Cantwell made herself a cup of tea and sat on the couch, looking out the window. During the limbo of mid-morning, nearly everyone was safely ensconced at work, and even the squirrels and blue jays on the nearby trees had disappeared. Wondering if they were all attending some faculty meeting in the hollow of the giant oak, she started to giggle. The giggle turned into a chortle, then a guffaw that segued into a snort. She didn't stop for a full minute, and then she had to calm herself down. When she finally surfaced, she gulped some tea to steady herself but kept to the couch and her view. At lunchtime, she made herself a tuna fish sandwich and retired afterwards for a little nap.

That evening, the phone rang repeatedly until she took the receiver off the hook.

By Monday, she had recovered sufficiently to start looking for some other type of work. But tenured and promoted as she was, she was badly out of practice. At the moment of her departure, she had merely thought, "Out." Since then, she had entertained thoughts of taking the corporate world by storm. But the employment ads from Sunday's paper looked so unpromising. Her first lead, manager for a database company, foundered when she called up and was told that she lacked the experience required. Her second shot, advertising executive, ran into similar difficulties. For a while, her days were dominated by disappointed inquiries and myriad cups of tea.

Somewhere in the middle, her department chair called to express concern. "What exactly happened on Thursday, Irene? I've been trying to reach you for days."

"Hmm. Phone trouble, I guess." She waved negligently, as if the phone had an optic pick up.

"Well, the dean's been on my case, and I had no idea what to tell him." A studied pause emanated from his end of the line. "Look, are you all right?"

"Never better." She tried to sound cheerful but it came out vacuous.

"Really. Do you want to talk about it?" For the last four years, the chair had been a fussy little man named Bramley, who matched his fingertips together when he talked from behind his desk. She could envision him doing so now.

"No, I don't think so." She twiddled her thumbs, pleased at their articulation. But realizing she had to say something more, she added, "I'll get back to you about this later, okay?"

By mid-week, she had decided to try volunteer work. But her stint at Literacy Helpers she found unutterably depressing. Most of the recipients didn't want to be there, and morale among the workers was low. Too much like her previous existence, she decided, and left the next day.

But what *was* she qualified for? Shaw's annoying epigram kept coming back to her like a Cheshire smirk: "He who can, does. He who cannot, teaches." For two full days, she decided she was going to write, but accomplished no more than opening paragraphs without follow-ups.

By the beginning of the third week, she began to grow lonely. Never an outgoing presence on the faculty, she had cultivated few friends, and her sole diversion had shrunk to Bramley's phone calls, which occurred almost daily at four o'clock, and whose poignant import could be summed up in two words: "Come back."

Her last attempt at independence was to invest half her savings in a pharmaceutical company lately in the news for developing an arthritis drug. But no sooner had she thrown her money into the ring than the company announced three serious drawbacks to the medication, the most serious of which was that it didn't work for most people, so she sold her plummeting shares, taking a healthy loss.

By the third Thursday after her departure, her inner calm had turned all fidgety. She was looking out the window for the fortieth time that morning, twiddling and untwiddling her thumbs, when she came to a decision as abrupt as her earlier resolution.

She got up, brushed the crumbs from breakfast off her skirt, and left the apartment. Driving at a safe five miles over the speed limit, she got to school by nine-thirty and parked in her usual space. She arrived at room 404A just as Professor Sexton, a bearded Victorianist who'd clearly been pressed into service to cover for her, was lecturing on Emerson. Owing to an academic time warp or the fact that Professor Sexton was out of his specialty, he had just gotten to the transcendentalists.

Professor Cantwell coughed peremptorily, interrupting Sexton's drone, and took over for him in mid-sentence. The class looked quite relieved, unless it was her imagination, and for the first time in a while Professor Cantwell felt in the right place. As for Sexton, he was not a Victorianist for nothing. With a gentlemanly bow, he picked up his notes and eased himself out of the classroom.

Professor Cantwell barely glanced in his direction. She had assigned Emerson's essay on self-reliance and intended to pursue it. Clearing her throat, she asked one of the students in the back row for a definition of the term.

# The Adjuster

Happy families are all alike; every unhappy family is unhappy in its own way. A blind overstatement, as Berger Bergson had once written in *The Aphorist*, a semi-annual organ of his own devising that now cluttered the periodical shelves of research libraries across the country. Happy families were happy because of wealth or welfare, the same aspects, in fact, that provoked unhappiness: a husband and wife whose money pushed them apart, or a child who fantasized about life outside the warm cocoon.

This damnable duality, the messiness of life itself, was the reason that most aphorisms were clever lies. In their urge toward the shapely utterance, they invariably falsified half of existence. Why couldn't novelists leave such philosophy to the sociologists or some other equally determined group? Did Tolstoy even believe what he wrote? Or was it simply novelistically convenient?

Had Berger Bergson lived in the sixteenth century, he would have sharpened his quill at this stage. Instead, as the year was 1948, he slammed the carriage return on his battered Royal typewriter and contemplated the accumulation of detritus that had fallen between the keys: pink eraser particles like the shavings from a pig, an apple seed, a nimbus of gray dust. It was on these staircase keys that he had composed his one and only novel, *The Realm of the Coin*, a pseudo Marxist, absurdist, hobbled fable in which no one won and the only hero was money.

He had been teaching freshman composition at Charleston College for chump change, he and Olga living literally on the other side of the tracks amid a welter of shacks like collapsed milk cartons and trailers propped on cinder blocks. Their neighbors were the enemy, either shouting and thumping each other or playing loud music to drown out everything else, as he labored nightly up and down the scale of the typewriter. During the day, with Berger at work, Olga used the typewriter to compose reports for a local insurance company, and he fancied that the daytime material somehow seeped into his acts of creation. His son Benjamin hadn't come along until later, in another town with Berger working another crummy teaching job and Olga helping out at an accountant's office.

Berger still had dreams and a head of brilliant black hair in those middle years. He didn't blame his students for dragging him down to the lowest common denominator of English, but rather felt inspired to be teaching America's youth. Having missed the war from acute bouts of tinnitus, he was now atoning in the academic trenches. On the side, he penned book reviews in the style of Randall Jarrell, a minor hero of his who was soon to write *Pictures from an Institution*.

*

The years passed like leaves blown into the gutter. Berger's novel was printed by a small New York publisher, achieved two reviews damning in opposite directions, and died in remainders. Now he was teaching Introduction to Literature, a step up from Composition, but to the same boneheaded students who couldn't tell Shakespeare from shinola. Raising Benjamin took all of Olga's time and half her looks, along with most of Berger's patience and a lot of his hair. The evening typing sessions became exercises in fighting off fatigue. "The pram in the corridor," Cyril Connolly had written sourly, "is the enemy of art." In the middle of teaching Dickens,

Berger dreamed of the Victorians and their practice of swaddling infants, dousing them with laudanum and hanging them from a convenient hook on the wall.

The G.I. bill had flooded the country with students wise beyond their years, veterans who knew someone like Chaucer's wife of Bath and thought *Romeo and Juliet* hootingly naive. Some just wanted to get their degrees and get the hell out, but others asked tough questions. One persistent nudger, a man named Levine who wore battle fatigues to class, perhaps gave Berger the idea for his obsession when he stayed for an hour after class to discuss just what Fitzgerald meant by "There are no second acts in American lives."

"That's not now it works," stated Levine finally, despite all of Berger's careful explanations about success and failure. He set his cap at a more defiant angle. "If a man blows it—I mean, really screws up—hell, he can always pull up stakes and settle in another town. That's what America's all about."

Berger realized that Levine was right, though all he said to him was "You may have a point." But did that invalidate Fitzgerald's fiction? That night, he did a lot of figurative head scratching as Olga put Benjamin to bed, then *he* put Benjamin to bed, then both went into Benjamin's room to reassure him that Mommy and Daddy weren't dead, after which Berger retreated to his typing and Olga took up anything but.

"To marry is to halve your rights and double your duties," thought Berger, who'd lately been dipping into Schopenhauer. Just a few years earlier, he'd immersed himself in Goethe and the eternal feminine that draws man ever upwards. Leaning back (the typing room was the bedroom, which adjoined the so-called living room), he took in Olga's thickening waist and ankles, the bluish look about her eye sockets, and the drab conversation to which they'd descended. Tomorrow morning, Benjamin would bang on his high chair for more grits, a South Carolina staple that they ate because they were currently residing in Charleston, where they lived because that was where Berger had procured his latest job. Olga was gradually losing faith in him, he could tell.

"You want any more pot roast?" She asked, he knew, because she wanted the last piece. These days she took solace in food, and who was he to deny her?

"No...thank you. I have had a sufficiency." He liked to employ ornate diction from time to time, like a shy person trying on a costume at home. Olga said nothing but merely shuffled into the kitchen. In another hour or so, she'd be asleep. He felt he should say something consoling but felt trapped himself. Tomorrow Benjamin would be up at six, Olga would take him to a woman across town by eight, and then she would go to work herself. Berger had no classes until nine, but he needed some time to collect his thoughts over a cup of coffee, and maybe get to the library first for an article he was planning on Thackeray. He'd had time to pursue only a master's degree, but he dreamed of attaining his doctorate or the equivalent by out-publishing the professors, as Housman had. In fact, he'd produced two pieces already, a short and perceptive essay on Swift and a learned query about *The Dunciad*. Like Pope, he yearned to push back dull chaos, but he found it slow going. He had no patron, and his muse was picking at pot roast.

Olga sighed from the kitchen like a wounded steam kettle. Benjamin wailed something indecipherable in his sleep. At this point, Tolstoy's dictum about families floated back to Berger. He snorted. Happy families—what on earth did Tolstoy know of such situations? Or Berger's own domestic arrangements, for that matter? What gave him the right to pontificate from his royal Russian ottoman?

So Berger started typing a few indignantly pedantic sentences about the opening of *Anna Karenina*. "'Happy families are all alike' is exactly what only an outsider with limited knowledge can claim. Unhappy families may seem different because of the variety of ills that plague humankind. Indeed, one can—"

"Want a cup of tea?" Olga's voice was inviting, and he knew that she just wanted company.

"You'd like me to, so I believe I will." Happy or unhappy? True or false? So many ambiguities in all directions.

Berger heard her drag the whining three-legged stool over to the cabinet to reach for the box of tea bags. This kitchen, low-ceilinged as the brow of an idiot child, nonetheless had cabinets suspended beyond Olga's grasp—*or what's a heaven for?* thought Berger klangily. Poor design, cheap construction. This kind of living cramped everyone in subtly hurtful ways: a sharper retort because of a shin barked on a narrow doorway, a vague anxiety unassuaged by the brick-wall view out the window. "Money is like a sixth sense without which you cannot fully enjoy the other five": Maugham's *Of Human Bondage*. Some bitter truth in that, so better leave it alone.

If it came to that, Berger's own childhood had brooked the commonest of poverty induced gloom, first in a tenement with Bergson Senior working as a tailor's assistant, later in a longer but narrower apartment when his father opened his own shop and swept home in a film of irritation every night. Berger feared castration from the patriarchal scissors, the *snip snip* still invading his dreams over three decades later. He was protected by the strong arms of his mother, who couldn't defend herself from the ravages of a stroke. His father had died in the black depths of 1943, convinced that the Allies would lose the war. Berger had only one sibling, his brother Ralph in upstate New York, who wrote him a card every Christmas.

\*

Olga brought two mugs of hot water and one tea bag, which she sloshed back and forth equitably until a brown stain had invaded both limpid pools. Olga still drank it with a little jam, the way her Ukrainian grandmother had. Berger sipped his plain.

Olga pressed her temples. "Benjamin was tough tonight."

"Hmm," Berger tilted his cup. "Maybe by the time he's twenty...."

She grinned crookedly, a raspberry pip from the jam stuck between her teeth. Every once in a while he could see traces of the old Olga, like a poorly scraped palimpsest. *And what's still visible of me?* he wondered, but said nothing. Instead, he contented himself by massaging some of the fatigue from his wife's shoulders with his adamant typing fingers. She sighed in pleasure, gave him a kiss, and soon trundled off to bed. She knew better than to insist he keep the same hours.

But after Olga had gone to sleep, he found that his creative facility had dozed off, as well. Were he, Benjamin, and Olga a happy family by any definition? Tolstoy, Schmolstoy! What he really wanted to type was more like this: "Happiness isn't more alike than any other category, from elephants to epiphanies. But isn't it just like a Russian soul to privilege suffering and its supposed unique aspects? In fact, the neurotic misery that plagues so many households is tediously familiar—but that wouldn't make much of a Russian novel, would it?" More in this vein would come to him three days later, after a particularly dyspeptic meal of corned beef and cabbage.

Thus Berger, entering a new trajectory. The next time, he attacked Thackeray and his declarations about women and weddings ("A woman with fair opportunities, and with an absolute hump, may marry WHOM SHE LIKES"). "Far truer for men than women," he observed sourly. Then, for reasons best known to his unconscious, it was on to Hemingway's prescription sedulously copied by would-be novelists everywhere, "Show—don't tell." "Why do so many solemn dicta of authors resemble nothing so much as flattering descriptions of how they write?" he typed indignantly. "Anyone who considered the matter for even a hairsbreadth would realize that almost all fiction contains elements of show and tell." That Henry James might have been there before Papa—Berger couldn't find the quotation, simply knew of it—simply set him against The Master, as well. "A drawing-room sensibility, that's what James had," he wrote decisively. "He sat at the table and told more than he ever showed, anyway. Not that he had much to show."

Berger found this kind of excoriating exercise liberating, even as it took him further and further away from his own literary praxis. Fortified by an extra cup of instant coffee after everyone else was asleep, he would straddle a chair Marlene Dietrich-style and go to town. One night, he conjured up a clutch of proverbs and had them war with one another: "He who hesitates is lost" versus "Look before you leap," "Too many cooks spoil the broth" versus "Many light hands make light work," and "Clothes make the man" versus "You can't judge a book by its cover."

When Benjamin began to copy his father's critical scowl and Berger frowned back, Olga told him reassuringly, "Imitation is the sincerest form of flattery."

"Hmph." Berger thought for only a second—and scowled. "Monkey see, monkey do." He regretted the incident, though not the proverbial weakness it exposed. Absence makes the heart grow fonder? Out of sight, out of mind. Seeing is believing? All that glitters is not gold. Make hay while the sun shines? Take time to smell the roses. Settled into a sort of rhythm, he produced a body of commentary-slash-invective (at times simply slashing invective) that ran to pages and pages. He polished it to a lapidary gloss, appended a throat-clearing introduction, and sent it off to a journal devoted to language and usage. It was returned with surprising promptness, and Berger spent that evening reviling shortsighted editors.

At an earlier stage in his career, he might have contented himself with scorn, but this time he decided to go public. Placing a small notice in *The New York Times Book Review*, he projected the inauguration of a journal called *The Aphorist*, soliciting funds for the first issue. This era was rife with little magazines, each clamoring to be heard, and nothing might have come of it but for the odd bequest of a recently deceased belle-lettrist named Henry Tryphus.

Tryphus was the eccentric author of such works as *Wit without Wisdom*, a collection of aphorisms, and *Wilde at Heart*, an examination of the Gay Nineties. His trademark was a finicky attention to detail approaching scholarship, though he seemed unappreciated by both the poets and the critics. After he died of an aneurysm in his early fifties, Tryphus was a dead eccentric author, his small share of posterity slowly metamorphosing into oblivion like a tree fossilizing into rock. (Berger checked, but nothing was even remotely in print.) His writerly output might have lived on in pitiful remainders, except that he'd been a man of some means, and his wife Emily had been entrusted with the task of popularizing his work. She seemed to think that *The Aphorist* was a suitable vehicle to bring her husband back from the dead.

"The elusive spirit of the epigram was behind all that my husband penned," wrote Mrs. Tryphus, from a well-appointed address in Boston. "I wonder whether yours isn't the guiding spirit to herald his genius and [something indecipherable]. I would, of course, provide a stipend and maybe even an [another blot] for the journal." Berger pictured a short, squat widow of the Arnold Bennett persuasion, pressing the point of her silver-nibbed pen too hard at critical junctures, perhaps when looking up at her husband's photo or merely pausing at some syntactical crossroad, causing a tiny eddy of ink to obscure certain words.

Berger wrote back in elaborately polite aposiopesis, expressing the hope that—it certainly seemed as if—but he had to confess that he was unfamiliar with her late husband's *oeuvre*, and if she would be so kind—.

She would. The next week, he received in the mail the complete works of Henry Tryphus, elegantly bound by a small New York press now as moribund as the author. Berger examined the slim volumes and read choice bits to his wife.

"Sounds like a long-lost relative of Max Beerbohm," remarked Olga, who wasn't Berger's helpmeet for nothing. Benjamin made funny faces with the rubber lips of a toddler.

"Intellectual curiosity will get you only so far," Tryphus had written, and "Greatness is no guarantee of goodness." Berger recognized the bite of true experience and kept his corrective mouth shut. Though Tryphus's work was rather uneven—he had a tendency toward prolixity when he got going—Berger decided he could live with this corpus. With a scholar's instinct for self-preservation, he chose not to gang up on his subject. Instead, he sent a flattering letter to Mrs. Tryphus, who wrote back delightedly, and over the course of six months, the journal began to take shape.

The school where he was currently teaching, Alameda U, was receptive to the idea. In fact, he suddenly acquired colleagues among the faculty, wishful academics who had a little something they'd been working on, a *feuilleton* on Twain's *Pudd'nhead Wilson* (maybe), or a query about a T. S. Eliot allusion (wrong journal). Berger enjoyed a raise, a shift to tenure track, and the illusion that he was liked at the university. He secured an office and some letterhead, installed Olga as his amanuensis, and set to work on the first issue.

Billing itself as a journal to celebrate the world's wisdom, *The Aphorist* devoted its first issue to Rochefoucauld, with a scrappy editorial about art and truth. "*Dans l'adversité de nos meilleurs amis,*" ran the banner around the cover, "*nous trouvons toujours quelque chose, qui ne nous déplaît pas.*" No accompanying translation. A thousand copies were printed in perfect bound signatures and sent to selected libraries across the country. The puff piece on Henry Tryphus was rigid with praise. Yet already Berger's real colors were visible under the stiff brocade: half the contents were devoted to Francophobia, including a haughty examination of Voltairean excess. Emily Tryphus was guardedly cordial, suspecting a quisling. Still, funds were advanced for the second issue, and in fact the Tryphusana Foundation was set up to allow unimpeded publication even after her death.

Meanwhile, life continued its errant course. In refutation of Hobbes (as Berger noted in issue three), it refused to be solitary, poor, nasty, brutish, and short, but rather grew increasingly like a crowded argument. As the Cold War heated up, Berger dared to print the Churchillian *bon mot*: "If a man is not a socialist at age twenty, he has no heart. If he is still one at age fifty, he has no head." Never mind that, as usual, Berger was only half in agreement with the idea—federal agents, or people calling themselves that, swooped into the Amadela English department and confiscated whole bales of the periodical. In the next issue, Berger chose to quote Auden's refutation of Shelley: "The unacknowledged legislators of the world are the secret police, not the poets."

At home and in the office, Olga played the loyal wife, editing her husband's rhetorical excesses when necessary and even coming up with some epigrams of her own: "Harm is where the art is" and, *pace* Chesterfield, "No man is a hero to his wife." Little Benjamin learned to recite a few apothegms, including one about children being unheard of and obscene, amusing any guests. For Berger now did have occasional callers, mainly tweedy professors with a few jottings, or arch pedants wishing to peddle their corrected views of literary history.

Also, Berger's teaching had grown more popular, tending to attract those students with literary pretensions. He even had groupies who hung about after class, waiting for a pearl to drop from his pursed lips and who tried to fit their own ungainly lives into the slender form of an epigram. One bright prospect, an M.A. candidate named Sid Connolly, a grim-faced type permanently wedded to a cigarette, was already working at *The Aphorist* as an assistant. The fifth issue carried a black-bannered editorial announcing that Emily Tryphus, patron saint of this periodical, was safely dead of a stroke—though not in those words.

During this time, Amadela's endowment had swelled with the advent of a new president, who had a flamboyant gift for soliciting wealthy alumni. More important personally, Berger had just been granted tenure and a substantial raise. He now had a real office with a window, a wedge of a desk, and a chair that reclined when he leaned back. The Bergsons had also moved to a better part of town and, at times, Berger felt affably affluent—a discomfiting feeling for an ex Marxist.

Still, "If you have a niche, scratch it," as he wrote in *The Aphorist* under the nom de plume "E. P. Gramme." This tone showed the journal with its feet up on a cracker barrel, chewing a hayseed. The journal was also capable of withering academic attacks, and an early defining moment came when it took on the *Partisan Review* in a dispute over the adages of left wing politics and post-Stalinist Russia. "All Berger Bergson did was prove himself right," sniped Mary McCarthy in an article written for a third periodical. Still, if any publicity is good publicity (a sentiment that Berger quarreled with in issue #7), *The Aphorist* had acquired a certain measure of renown. An increasing amount of what would have been Olga's time, were it not for Sid, went into filling subscription orders and answering correspondence.

Berger's reputation wasn't quite big enough to move to New York, but was swollen enough to occupy whatever space it was given on campus. He encouraged a bright and shapely acolyte named Pamela, who never quite slept with him. Concurrently Olga had an affair with a colleague of Berger's, a suave Renaissance expert who talked of Donne and Jonson as if they were pals of his. Berger didn't learn about the liaison until years afterwards, when it was too late to do anything about it but drink.

In the Sixties, the Alameda students protested the war with a five-day sit-in at the Student Center, an adolescent Benjamin worried about the draft and decided to puncture his eardrums with a pencil, and Olga raised her vaginal consciousness in the company of six other women and a speculum. Appalled, intrigued, enraged, Berger threw darts in many directions, devoting an entire issue to tearing down Chairman Mao's Little Red Book. He pointed out how Malcolm X's "If you're not part of the solution, you're part of the problem" corresponded eerily to Christ's "Those who are not with me are against me." By now, he (or Sid and his successors) had filled a massive file cabinet with two sets of entries, one organized according to subject and the other in first-main-word alphabetization.

*The Aphorist* had always been a journal veering between eighteenth-century coffeehouse repartee, a modern insistence on tough reasonableness, and the black velvet backdrop of nihilism. "Things aren't the way they used to be," proclaimed one famous editorial, "and probably never were." But the greater the accumulation of massed wisdom, the more pressure on the foundation. All those apothegms, repartee, *bon mots*, aphorisms, epigrams, adages, mottos, and witticisms began to sound alike, repetition with minor variations, cleverness spread over the appalling wound of experience. His *Bartlett's Familiar Quotations* lay in shreds. Berger leaned back in his swivel chair and wondered: Was truth a mere matter of phrasing?

So in the Seventies, Berger entered the treacherous realm of paradox. "All generalities are false." "Every rule has an exception." *Ad nauseam.* Seemingly overnight, his hair grew grizzled and his step acquired a wariness as if he were treading on rotten floorboards. He developed a cardiac arrhythmia that he was told to keep an eye on.

And what of Olga, his staunch helpmeet? *Was beauty only skin-deep?* he would muse after hearing a recumbent snore (he still went to sleep a mile after the rest of the household), or did Keats have it right when he proclaimed, "A thing of beauty is a joy forever"? Describe *beauty*. Define *joy*. *Olga*, he whispered to her presiding spirit as her corporeal essence slumbered on, *how long is forever?* Olga left him in 1975 after two more affairs, the last so indiscreet that colleagues sniggered in the hallways. One year earlier, Benjamin had finally departed for college up north. The family had for years been unhappy in numbingly familiar ways.

Increasingly, Berger sat at his desk and sulked. Thoreau had written, "Most men lead lives of quiet desperation." But what of the noisy complainers who filled his days? "Whereof one cannot speak, thereof one must be silent." Wittgenstein: the last sentence of *Tractatus*. But the same objection held: many pseudo-pundits made a living pontificating on subjects they in fact knew little about. Everyone from the English department chair to the students had claims on his attention, opinions to spout.

In the greedy Eighties, Berger succumbed to surfeit, and on certain days he felt like saying nothing more complex than "May I have a glass of water, please?" Benjamin had just re entered medical school after two false attempts, and Olga was writing a memoir called *As I Lay Lying*. But Berger's main job was still pedagogy. Currently he was teaching a British literature survey course and re-encountering *Hamlet* for the first time in decades. He found, like T. S. Eliot before him, that Hamlet doth protest too much and was thinking of linking the melancholy Dane (who was, after all, a Wittenburg graduate student) with some of the current crop of masters candidates.

"But when Polonius says, 'This above all, / To thine own self be true,'" protested a young man with a goatee and a scowl (they were all young, now that Berger had turned sixty-five), "what are we supposed to make of that? Isn't the old guy a fool or something?" Berger recognized an heir to Levine, the ex-G.I. who had objected to Fitzgerald and thus spurred Berger on his quest: he had the same querulous tone, the same suspicion of received wisdom that was at first refreshing but soon enough tiresome. And Berger was quite tired that day, having dealt with the dean of liberal arts, a stack of essays, and an ex-wife who wanted more alimony.

"That depends," countered Berger, to buy time. Only after class, as he attempted to impart some words of wisdom to the young man, did he realize that he had become Polonius, giving flabby advice to rigid youth. "Wisdom comes with age," he thought as he piloted his aging Datsun home through the student-clogged avenues. But in the bent-over figure of a man with a cane negotiating the curb on Fanshaw Street, he saw an image of his father in old age, along with one of his father's lines, "No fool like an old fool." His father had been dead for decades, his mother more recently deceased, but his mind flew from their graves in New Jersey to their hardscrabble lives, and what they would think of their son these days. The year was 1984, shades of Orwell, himself a puncturer of others' ideological balloons. Berger felt a bit deflated himself, as if his skin were sagging all over.

At home, he made himself a dinner of leftover spaghetti. Then he set to work. Having traded an IBM Selectric for an IBM computer, he flicked on his screen and opened the latest file concerning *The Aphorist* and an editorial on Auden. In his old age, what he had of it, Auden dipped back into his anti-fascist poem "September 1, 1939" and altered a key line, "We must love one another or die." Disgusted by its romantic choice (concerning Yeats's agonized artist's dichotomy "forced to choose / Perfection of the life, or of the work," Auden wrote, "This is nonsense, we live in imperfection"), he went back to produce "We must love one another and die," arguing to anyone who'd listen that everyone dies anyway, love notwithstanding. But that didn't make as powerful a line, did it? No fool like an old fool.

Berger sat back after this deliverance, reflecting on his life and the character he had become. As Henry James said in "The Art of Fiction," "What is character but the determination of incident? What is incident but the illustration of character?" To hell with James. He sat hunched in a broken-slatted chair with a greatcoat mantling his shoulders like an image of Nietzsche, who had famously declared, "No true artist will tolerate for one minute the world as it is." Berger had endured his surroundings with the sour zeal of a monk. He annotated the Nietzsche quotation with a few sharp queries: "What is a true artist as opposed to a false one?" "Why the exaggeration 'one minute'?" "What is 'the world as it is' [incl. German?], anyway?" *Und so weiter.*

He was alone. Was that the true condition of life?

At this point, he got up and made himself a mug of tea with a sachet of Twinings Earl Gray. He recalled the double cup he used to share with Olga, swishing the one wet Tetley bag back and forth over two rims like a tongue over lips. We must love one another or die. Slowly he began to cry, a few fat tears plopping into his tea.

He reached out to take a salty sip, but the liquid seemed to have turned to ice, and a peculiar pain gripped his left arm. Then came a sudden blow as if an elephant had stamped on his chest. The mug fell to the floor and smashed, spreading a stain. He remembered what his cardiologist had told him and ignored the warning in the same angry thought. Returning to the keyboard was difficult, especially when the pain was getting worse, but he managed to type out some lines. "Death devours all lovely things. *Ugly ones, too.*" "Any man's death diminishes me. *Arrant egotism.*" His father's voice: "Now that's telling 'em." But Berger was growing faint, the screen flickering in front of him like a specter. Too late to change his life, as Rilke advised. Better to end this way.

The last line he typed, found by a scared undergraduate sent two days later to find what had happened to Professor Bergson, stretched back to Homer: "There is a time for many words, and there is also a time for sleep." That wasn't quite right, either, but there hadn't been time to adjust it.

# All You Can Eat

The young man placed his hands over the table, as if blessing the ham biscuits, deviled egg plate, pasta salads, green bean casserole, cocktail shrimp and at least a dozen other dishes. "Life," he pronounced, "is an endless cycle of choices and consequences."

"Not endless," said the old man beside him, his head shaking with a rhythm that might have been contrary or involuntary.

It was a potluck dinner to benefit the local parks commission, arranged by somebody's friend. Table space was short, so they ate off paper plates on their laps. An old-fashioned evening out, the young man had thought as he left his apartment with a bucket of potato salad and twenty bucks for a contribution. He was right in one way, he found, when the door opened at a house where the median age of guests was sixty-five. But he was ushered in before he could think of a way to beg off, and the door behind him seemed to have disappeared. Fifteen minutes later, he was poking at three-bean salad next to a man who might've reminded him of a beloved uncle, except that he had none, and his family was held together by tolerance, at best. Growing up, he'd nurtured an alienation that B+ types mistook for homegrown genius.

The young man took a bite of something orange and wiggly and began again. "Statistically, people make bad choices 75 percent of the time."

"You mean this cucumber salad?" A tremor passed through the old man's arm, causing some of his salad to slide onto the floor.

"I'll get that." The young man bent over to pinch it up with a napkin. The old man thanked him, but then seemed to lose focus. He was grappling with a chicken wing, which apparently made him unable to talk, maybe even think.

The young man had more or less given up on conversation anyway, but still had a few more philosophical remarks to unload. "If only we could marry ideas instead of people."

The words seemed to trigger the old man. He took a careful sip of wine and started talking about his dead wife, Mary. A flower in the asphalt of his life, he said, proof that true love still exists. The young man couldn't help but interrupt: "True love seems so miraculous because of all the times it doesn't work."

"Maybe, but Mary was different. We met at a supper like this. She smiled at me over a plate of home-baked rolls."

"Love at first bite, huh?" An easy joke he thought the geezer would appreciate. He continued, his mouth full of corn. "I had a girlfriend like that named Stacy, and it lasted all of three weeks."

"You don't understand. We were married for forty-two years."

"Jesus." The young man's idea of a relationship was more like texting on the weekdays and sexting on the weekends. Next Tuesday, one of them would dump the other. "I guess you can tell me all about suffering."

"Well, we didn't have much money, but we got by." His hand shook only slightly as he managed another sip of wine. "Loved her through thick and thin...."

The young man heard "sick and sin" and perked up a bit. Other people's pain took his mind off his own. But the old man was describing how he'd never been tempted by another, not when he had what he wanted.

"I want in seven different directions." The young man pointed all over the room, at a plate of brownies and a platter that had held lemon squares, but also at a cloisonné vase and a plump woman in sandals. "That's my problem in life."

"Your problem—" the old man admonished, but paused when the young man had ceased listening. He reached out to tap the young man on the shoulder but ended up shaking him. His hand had taken on an agitation of its own. "You just haven't tried the right dish."

What seemed like heartfelt motion got the young man's attention, and the words took on an oracular note. The young man traded in his plate for a new one and this time went for the ribs, tried the pepper slaw, even helped himself to something encased in cherry Jell-O. When he was finally done, he stared up at the room's faded chandelier, which looked like a crystal octopus. Each facet refracted dimly against another, the angles multiplying as if the universe were a chain of half-lit options. The light led him on, and eventually out the door. Long after he left the party and late on the street, the young man followed lampposts, passing through each yellow glow and lingering under the few outside darkened restaurants. He studied the menus posted behind glass and tried to take them all in. More? More. He'd sampled everything at the table. Now what?

# Question Authority

Amy was conceived by two irresponsible individuals, Doug and Dora, during a commercial break in Superbowl XIII. For weeks afterwards, they did nothing except nurture a sense of impending gloom. Abortion was out of the question because it was never asked.

"Biology is destiny," muttered Doug, quoting from something he'd learned in school.

Eventually, where the bottom of Dora's T-shirt and the top of her jeans didn't meet was a mile of beachfront. Anticipating future growth, they moved into a slightly larger apartment. Waiting for the event was like counting to one over and over. When the infant arrived, one Tuesday at four in the morning, they called her Amy the Accident.

"She's perfectly benign," claimed Dora.

"Like a tumor," said Doug.

Amy didn't understand, but she heard, all right. She rejected the breast in favor of the bottle. She perfected an accusing stare. Evenings she spent in her high chair, flicking apple goo at the walls. Some of it stuck. Her favorite object was a bunny chew-toy that wore a look of deep concern.

At the daycare facility, she learned to get attention by tripping people. At home, she practiced what she'd learned at daycare.

As Amy grew into a toddler, Doug and Dora began to drift away from each other like two unheavenly bodies.

"Be good," Dora told their daughter.

"Make sure someone else gets blamed," advised Doug.

"*Smile and wave*," Dora whispered when Amy tried to talk to the mailman, "but don't be too friendly. These people can't help you."

"Better to be pissed off than pissed on," Doug told her after she got angry over her toilet training.

Her grandparents sent thin checks.

Doug and Dora split up when Amy was five, and she shuttled between studio apartments in Chicago and New York for the next ten years. She would lie flat on her back on the cot provided by her father in Chicago, traveling in her mind, the water stain on the ceiling the last continent before sleep. Or she would stay awake in Queens, listening to her mother on the phone, cooing to some stranger who never panned out. Another fragile day.

At ten, she looked toward cops, teachers, and doctors as authority figures who might straighten her out. One check-up with the local internist lasted a suspiciously long time. The policeman sent her home. Eventually, she became another alienated teenager, wearing a T-shirt with the message "NOT INVOLVED." "You have an ounce of talent and a pound of brass," declared the drama teacher, who also complimented her tits. At fifteen, in a BMW 540, she made it with three guys who called themselves lawyers and gave her a hundred-dollar bill for her pains. At sixteen, she bolted but could think of nowhere to end up. Hitching toward Vegas, she overshot to a suburb thirty miles out, populated mainly by senior citizens. The town's main attractions were a boardwalk promenade over an artificial lake and what the oldsters called a brothel: Double Velvet, with a faded marquee sign that read, "The most delicious girls in the world!"

Amy tried to fit in, faking her age and going to work at the local industry. Her overslung figure was a metaphor for nothing but itself. The madame told her to cultivate a slightly hard to get air for better tips. So Amy learned to purse her lips and say, "I know what men like. And sometimes I give it to them." But mostly she faced a roomful of impatient people. She specialized in vices that couldn't be versaed. "Step on me as if you meant it," one man told her, so she did.

It was all too, too stupid-making, though she was earning decent money. And delight needs tedium, she learned.

One night she was in that rare mood where everyone looks lovely because they're human. An almost absurdly tall man stood drinkless at the bar. He was wearing a uniform compounded of two parts authority and one part masculine vigor, and looked like the man she'd sought in her childhood dreams. She sidled up to him, slightly tongue-tied.

"I'm."

"You're."

What followed was not an important silence. His name, she eventually learned, was Daryl, and he leaned toward her like a mis-driven pole in the ground. She took him in hand.

In the bedroom, Amy knew, some men liked to talk, particularly about their wives, but Daryl was different. He was ready even before she was, his snakeskin boots off with a whuff of air that left her breathless. He put on two condoms for extra protection but seemed to be one of those men whose love goes all over the place. Long after it was time to stop, he paused.

"Sorry, you can't have any more sex," she told him gently. "There's none left." She pulled on her pair of so-tights, whereupon he began to beg.

So she did it again with him, this time without any protection, all the while wondering what the hell got into her. Was going to get into her. Had.

Zipping himself back into his uniform, he promised to return and rescue her. "From what?" she asked.

The next day, she hugged her belly before breakfast. But the hours lengthened into air as Daryl didn't reappear. All she retained was his first name and the odor of worn boots. She tried to track him down, but her man had evaporated. Two weeks later, she began feeling nauseated. She contemplated termination but decided against it. Then she thought of her unwanted childhood and headed to the clinic for a D&C.

She still works at the Double Velvet but won't go to bed with any man wearing boots. And when someone asks her to dress up in a uniform, she grows unaccountably shy.

# Zack and the Beanstalk

The first time the phone rang, Jill and I were out back, admiring the progress of a sweet basil plant that had outgrown its red clay flowerpot. We were already planning several jars of pesto sauce in the lazy way that a laundry load becomes a clean wash already folded and put away, though the clothes are still in the hamper. The phone rang from far away, like some tuneful but mechanical insect, and it was a while before either of us realized what it was. By the time Jill ran in to get it, the caller had hung up. Coming back out, she put on a little girl's frown.

"Never mind," I said sensibly. "If it was important, they'll call back."

We've been married for five years, and living in Mississippi for three of them. Jill always gets to the phone first on the off chance that it's someone offering a job or claiming us as sweepstakes winners, enabling us to move back to the Northeast, which is where Jill rightfully belongs. She's not a hothouse blossom but a sturdier growth, suited to a cold-weather climate. She also gave up a promising career in editing to follow me down here, as she often reminds me. But I teach English at the state university in Starkville, which is where I got a job after leaving graduate school. What started out as a temporary post has stretched into an endless perennial, renewed at the end of every academic year. I dutifully send out my curriculum vitae, but so far I've had no luck. Meanwhile, we've made a few friends on the faculty, invested in a hammock, and planted a garden. Sometimes the difference between an act of optimism and one of desperation is simply one of emphasis.

Later that evening, after a coiled-up dinner of spaghetti and canned sauce, the phone rang again. The water was running in the sink, and Jill was wearing what I call her proctologist's gloves, but she managed to strip them off and reach the phone in under three rings.

"Hello? Oh, hi," she told the receiver tucked between her shoulder and neck, as I came into the kitchen. *It's Zack*, she mouthed at me, as she walked slowly back to the sink, stretching the cord. Zack Bertrand is one of our senior faculty members, though not to be confused with the Old Fossils, who've been here forever and will soon retire, possibly horizontally. Zack is a native New Yorker, *né* Zachary, so of course Jill told him we were urban types. He's been down here fifteen years, during which time he's bought a house and turned interior decorator. He's always busy re-sanding his deck, pruning his bamboo grove, or acquiring more artwork for his living room. His slightly prim, fussy demeanor made Jill label him an old maid as soon as she met him. But his enthusiasms, from French cooking to film noir, make him lively company. More important, he invited us to dinner soon after we arrived, and we've been friends ever since.

"Really?" said Jill as she turned the hot-water tap back on stealthily. Zack tends toward logorrhea, especially on the phone, proposing and answering his own questions. "A night-blue what? That's amazing." She reached for one of the dinner dishes and began to rinse it. I backed away—this sounded like one of Zack's longer perorations—and went into the living room to grade a set of papers. By the time Jill got off the phone, it was after nine o'clock, though I'd marked only half the set. Grading should get easier over time, but instead it just seems to get more involved. And since the next semester's students don't magically learn from the last group I taught, every year is a painfully fresh beginning, with the same mistakes and false starts. In some ways, it's like a marriage.

"Zack was on a roll tonight," said Jill, when she finally emerged from the kitchen. "Ever hear of a night-blooming cereus?"

"Um, no. Should I have?"

Jill cocked her head. "They're not that common. But Zack has one. He says it blooms once a season, but at night, and only during a full moon. Isn't that weird?"

I had visions of a pale pink blossom with delicate feminine features. Did Zack play music to it, and if so, what kind? *Blue Moon? Moonlight Serenade?* I turned toward the back window, where a three-quarter moon hung low in the sky, bulging against a silver blanket of cloud. "So when's it due?" I asked.

"Well, that's just it." Jill draped her hands on my shoulders, kneading slightly. When we haven't been feeling particularly intimate—which is lately all the time—we try to make up for it with little physical gestures. At least, that's what the counselor told us to do. "It could be any day now, and he wants to invite us over for the viewing."

"*Hmmm.*" This was more in response to Jill's massage than to Zack's invitation. Hunching over a stack of papers always makes my back ache. When her thumbs dug gently into my shoulder blades, I grunted in pleasure. "Sure...*unh*...I'd be...*mmm*...interested. What do we have to do?"

"Just sit tight. He'll call us." Jill slid her hands down to my lower back and even lower, until I couldn't stay still any longer and reached back to cup her right breast. I caressed the soft underflesh till the nipple grew hard. Slowly and precisely I unbuttoned her blouse. We ended up on the couch, whose resilient tan cushions give the feel of a third body. And we made love, though there was something too deliberate about the act. For the past year, Jill had been trying to conceive. We had intercourse two or three times a week—in bed, on the rug, in both orthodox and strange positions—but nothing seemed to work. My private theory was that there'd be no conception till we were really friendly again. And I didn't see that happening until we moved away from this dry zone.

For some reason we kept putting off any clinical tests, though I could tell Jill was getting impatient. At the moment there was no blame assigned, though sometimes she accused me of feeling ambivalent about the whole business, and sometimes she was right. Meanwhile we just kept having at it in what I called "trying circumstances." We went to sleep soon afterwards, lying in parallel lines. In the morning I drove off to teach, and Jill worked on a freelance writing assignment she'd wangled from an editor she knew at *Cosmopolitan*. The subject was "10 Great New Ways to Make Love."

Five days later, at ten in the evening, we got another call from Zack. This one I fielded, simply because I was right by the phone, headed toward the refrigerator to scrounge. "Hey, kiddo!" came Zack's voice from the other side of town. In Zack's parlance, men are kiddos and women are dears.

"Hey, Zack. What's up?" I prepared myself for a long conversation.

"It's here! My cereus has bloomed. You have to come over right away."

"Um, okay, I guess. Should we—"

"Yes, good. Tell Jill to bring her camera." And with that, he hung up.

The moon hung like some ethereal grapefruit as we drove the mile to Zack's house. We said nothing to break the darkness between us. Jill had her Minolta in a black cloth bag, and at the last minute I'd brought along a bottle of Beaujolais. Zack had a capacity for ceremony that seemed vaguely entwined with his Catholicism, though he rarely spoke about religion.

"Do you suppose he has a name for it?" asked Jill as we got out of the car. Almost all the lights were off in Zack's house, possibly in deference to the natural moon-glow.

"I don't know, but maybe this isn't the right plant."

"What do you mean?" Suddenly she looked quite concerned. "This isn't the kind of thing that Zack makes up."

"Maybe, maybe not." I smiled so that only the darkness could see as I rang the bell. "I think I'll just march up to this blossom and say, 'Surely, you can't be cereus.'"

Jill nudged me hard in the ribs as Zack opened the door. He was wearing a black plaid vest and what I can describe only as a maternal look.

"Come in, come in." He took my bottle and thanked me. "We'll have this another time. I've made a pitcher of martinis. It's out on the deck."

We followed in silence, past the reproduction of Michelangelo's *David*, through Zack's study with its computer covered by a giant tea cozy. In the semi-dark, all the furniture looked sharp and angular, tables encroaching on chairs, cabinets projecting into the wall. Zack slid open the glass door to the porch, and the mood was such that we all tiptoed outside. It was a warm evening, though already mid-September.

"My God," I whispered, "it's so big!"

We stared at the white globe of a blossom, the size of a baby's head, connected to the trunk by a sinuous, fleshy-green stalk. "It looks alive," sighed Jill wonderingly.

"Well it *is* alive," pointed out Zack pedantically. "If you look here, you can see—"

"No, I mean—breathing or something. Like an animal."

"It's just so big," I repeated stupidly. It looked like something in a fairy tale, what you climb to reach the giant, maybe.

The blossom itself was about six inches in diameter, like a huge milky wine glass set to catch moon rays. In point of fact, the flower wasn't moving at all, but I could see what Jill meant. The soft, overlapping petals seemed to form an open diaphragm, motionlessly taking in the still night air. Poking up at its base was a snakelike greenish stamen. Zack's night-blooming cereus, I couldn't help thinking, was a hermaphrodite.

"Georgia O'Keefe never painted anything like this," I murmured.

"No, I don't think so," said Zack over the *chink-a-chunk* of ice falling into three glasses as he precisely poured the martinis. Jill was slowly, almost dreamily setting up her camera. "But Robert Hayden wrote a poem about one."

When she'd finished, we raised our glasses and pronounced "A toast to all," the drinking phrase Zack used for all occasions. The martinis were like an icy floe of gin, relieved by a whisper of vermouth but also something else, some indefinable evergreen essence. The juniper in the gin, maybe.

The cereus should also be given a glass, I thought. "Does it need any water?" I asked, feeling as if I should be addressing the plant.

Jill stepped in front of the naked bloom. "I can go get some," she volunteered.

"Or I could—" began Zack.

"Zack and Jill went up the hill to fetch a pail of water...." I recited.

"—but I don't think it needs any," Zack concluded, not responding to my joke.

"I'm not sure these photos are working," announced Jill some ten minutes later. She rose from her squat on the deck, a last attempt to get a close-up of the flower. "Moonlight is tricky that way." She took a last gulp from her martini glass, crunching the weak ice.

"Would you like a refill?" Zack was a concerned host. "There's another pitcher in the fridge."

"I'll go get it." But walking back through Zack's study, I caught sight of a Robert Hayden volume that he'd left on the desk. I picked up the book and idly flipped through it, looking for the poem he'd mentioned. Before I found it, out popped a letter addressed to "My dearest Zack."

I drew back for a second. This was private. Oh, what the hell, I thought, smothering my guilt. The handwriting was back-slanted, the message rather perfumed. Midway through, the letter waxed poetic over the Platonic joys of a blow job. It was signed, "Your very own—love, Ernest." The address was in Memphis.

Well. So Zack had something going on the side. Good for him, I thought. Good that he has a real life, even if it's not one he cares to share with anyone around here. I carefully replaced the letter and tiptoed out.

"Did you find the pitcher all right, kiddo?" Zack looked slightly concerned, and I realized that I'd forgotten the damned thing after I put it down in Zack's study.

"But Jill was taking the pitcher," I said, attempting a recovery. "Just kidding—I left it in one of the rooms."

Zack nodded as if he also left pitchers lying around the house. His expression now seemed to me somewhat sensual, those pursed lips now bunched for a kiss, the fluttering hands ready to alight on someone's thigh. I wondered for an instant what it would be like, then dismissed the scene. In the kitchen, I quickly found a reserve half-pitcher of martinis in the refrigerator and sloshed it into the one I held.

All of us had another round and sipped contemplatively for a while. Up above, the moon was beginning to edge toward the horizon. Zack suddenly looked agitated, as if aware that the evening was slipping from him. "Tell you what—how about a picture with all of us around the cereus?"

"Someone's got to hold the camera," I pointed out.

"Why?" Zack almost pouted. "Doesn't it have a timer?"

"Well, it does." Jill began fiddling with the mechanism. "I can try, anyway." She set up the Minolta on the ledge of the deck, peering through the viewfinder. Then she had us gather around the cereus as if we were playing a game of ring-around-the-rosy. A moment's dart to the camera to set the timer brought her back at once. "All right, we've got ten seconds. Get ready, smile...."

I had one hand on Zack's shoulder and the other chastely around Jill's waist. The click of the camera caught Zack blinking and me with a forced smile. "Try again?" I suggested.

This time, I switched from Zack's shoulder and Jill's waist to Zack's waist and Jill's shoulder. But as Zack leaned into my arm, something wooden gave behind me with a crack, and Zack disappeared into the shrubbery.

"Aaaah...hell!" The rotten railing of the deck had given way, and Zack was prostrate on an azalea bush. In a moment, he flopped over to the ground.

"God, Zack, are you all right?"

"I...think so." He felt himself. "More the shock than anything."

"But you're bleeding," Jill pointed out. It was true: the sharply trimmed branches of the azalea had pierced the back of his vest in several places, and blood oozed through.

I headed for the sliding door. "Where do you keep your bandages?"

"In the medicine cabinet...." Zack gestured helplessly.

I found a tin of Band-Aids in the bathroom and some paper towels in the kitchen, one of which I wet with soap and water. When I got back, Zack was gingerly removing his vest. It looked as if someone had thrown strawberries at his back.

"Ow...*ow!*" Zack winced as Jill started dabbing at the cuts.

"You're in luck," I told Zack, as I inspected where the railing had collapsed. "It looks like one rotten board."

"I'll have to check all of them." Zack sighed wearily. "Or get someone to do it."

After Jill had neatly bandaged Zack in three places, she started packing up her camera equipment. He asked her again about the photos.

"We'll just have to see how they come out," she told him. "Sometimes you get pleasantly surprised."

"Life," proclaimed Zack, "can be full of pleasant surprises. Ouch."

"What'd you have in mind?" Jill, I could tell, was thinking of some gratifying event that would magically land us out of Mississippi. I felt an irrational impulse to kick her, to push her through the hole in the railing into the prickly azalea bush.

Zack waved his hands again. "Oh, I don't know...friends dropping in, enjoying a good drink." He gestured toward the cereus for the tenth time that night. "Seeing a night-blooming cereus." For a moment, we all looked at it again as if for the first time. Was that a little bow it took, or just the breeze?

"Actually, it reminds me of *The Little Shop of Horrors*," said Jill, breaking the spell. "That huge man-eating plant—what was its name? Seymour?"

"No, my dear, Seymour was the man who fed it. I saw the film twice." Zack looked into the middle distance in endless rerun. He tilted his glass, but it was empty.

"It's late." She yawned quietly, turning to me. "You've got to teach tomorrow. We really should go."

I opened my mouth and shut it.

"Not another drink?" Zack cocked his head toward the kitchen. "I have some homemade madeleines I could offer you."

"No, thanks." Jill checked her watch by the light of the moon. "We've really got to leave."

"All right, if you must." Zack was downcast but gallant. "I'll pack up two Proustian madeleines to go."

In the kitchen, he carefully prepared a foil package. Before I knew it, we were out the door and driving down the block, with Zack waving goodbye from his porch. I thought we might quarrel any second, but I was wrong.

Jill bit her lip. "I always feel lonely after seeing him. His little rituals, him in that big house."

I was stopped at a traffic light throwing a green cone of light onto the pavement. "Has it ever occurred to you that he may be seeing someone?"

"What? Zack?"

"Someone in Tennessee, I believe." I was being deliberately off-hand, which I knew would annoy her.

"What are you talking about?"

"Just what I said. Zack. Is seeing. Someone."

Now she looked really upset. "When did he tell you this?"

"He didn't. I found a letter when I was getting that pitcher."

"It's not right to look at other people's mail, you know."

"I know. I couldn't help myself." I gestured at the nighttime sky. "I can be impetuous sometimes."

"Hmm." She shook her head reprovingly, then smiled. "Anyway. Is this person male or female?"

"Which do you think?"

"All right, but I hope he's not getting taken advantage of by some little blond boy."

"Yeah, me, too. Anyway, we can't ask him about it." We finished the drive in silence, both of us feeling rather protective of Zack. We made the final swerve onto our driveway under the light of the sunken moon, by now hidden between the trees.

When we got out, I fumbled long enough with the house key for Jill to reach past me with her own key. Her bare arm rubbed silkily against mine, first by accident, then again by design. The moonlight made her flesh glow, and suddenly I very much wanted to be inside that flesh. We didn't grope or kiss, but once we got inside, we simply walked to the bedroom and started taking off all our clothes. Vestiges of the moon peeked through the blinds as I parted Jill's thighs, and she grabbed me hard. For the first time in a while, our bodies fit together perfectly. When my arms snaked around her waist, she twisted me around with her hips. She ended up on top, riding me as I gripped her buttocks, all the way home and then some. That night, we slept better than we had in months.

*

The pictures of the plant came out well, all except the shots with the four of us. And of course there was one shot of a plant, two humans, and a missing railing, which might have been useful for insurance purposes. We sent copies to Zack wrapped in aluminum foil with "MADELEINE EXCHANGE" marked on the front. Two months later, Zack invited us to a dinner party at his place. It was too wintry for the deck, but Zack insisted on having a drink out there just to show us where the break had been repaired. It looked almost indistinguishable from the rest of the railing. The cereus lay withered in the corner, a set of lifeless stalks. Jill shivered, and when Zack politely asked if she were cold, Jill announced that she was pregnant.

"My goodness," said Zack. He turned to me. "And how do you feel about this?"

"I—I don't know." I looked at Jill, who had told me earlier that day, with the first of what were to be her secret inner smiles, as if having a wordless dialogue with the growing creature inside. "I've known about this for all of six hours. Relieved, I guess."

"Say congratulations." Zack looked a little prim. "It's your wife. It's your family."

I nodded wordlessly.

Jill reached over and laid her hand on mine. "That's all right. He's been quite helpful, really." Her manner was different from usual, as if her personality had added an overarching umbrella. She hadn't talked at all about moving lately. When I thought of the baby, all that came to mind was a curled-up fetus under a cabbage. When I thought of what this would do to us, I was half-grateful, half-terrified. Zack, I saw, was watching us both paternally.

"A toast to all," he intoned, holding up his glass. After a moment's hesitation, we raised ours, too.

# Returns

The Bar None in Bend, Idaho, has a welcoming committee of one drunk blonde named Elma, smarter than you think, who works on her comeback lines the way some women work on their nails. She has one of those so young, so old faces, and legs long enough to trap any man into conversation. "Living out my days, that's not enough," she remarks to the bartender, whose function in this piece is to be dead.

In walks a guy named Rob, who looks as if he specializes in the science of drab. Brown suit. He's the only customer in the bar besides Elma, leaving her little choice.

After a few minutes, she exhales a smoke ring that drifts over to his G&T. "I live a life of unrequited loathing."

He shakes his head, lightly ensnared in her smoke. "I don't want to be the beneficiary of your guilt."

She frowns at him. "Welcome to Never Mind Land." Then bares her armpits in a healthy, breast-lifting stretch. "You look so uninteresting, it's interesting. Some people have a pet goldfish. You probably have a pet peeve."

"Go ahead," he waves away the smoke as if it were tentacular, "summarize me."

"Okay." She welcomes the invitation. "You have the cheapest dreams."

"They kill the dwarves in my mind."

"You prefer forgetting to forgiving."

"Please," he says, in a non-pleasing manner, "if that's your hum, where's the dinger?"

Elma looks at him more closely. Her patented "one-two-three-flinch" routine isn't working. Decides to regroup. "Could I have another parasol for my drink?" she asks the dead bartender. "Mine's wilted." Turns back to the new guy. "So what were you saying?"

"What what?"

"That's a big what."

She sneers. "Wouldn't it be great if it were great?"

Like all males, he misinterprets *it*. Grins out of context and leans toward her. "Why didn't you say so? Insert me into slot A."

"You've got to be kidding." She extinguishes her cigarette in his drink. "Three hundred years later, the answer would still be no."

"Sure." He decides to save face. "Know what? Making love to you would be like climbing Mount Improbability."

"Here's some middle-aged wisdom." She crosses her legs like a scissors. "Settle for less."

"Maybe. What I don't have, I've got plenty of."

"So I see." She decides to turn the tables but settles for the bar-stool. "Okay, your turn. You're allowed one and a half questions."

"All right, here's a Zen koan. What's the taste of a tuna fish sandwich you didn't eat?"

A smile. "Something fishy about that."

"Deduct two points."

Her eyes widen. "No fair."

"Fuck you."

A pause. Another pause. "I could make an issue of it, but that would make it issue #327, and I've got to move on." She checks her watch, which was stolen yesterday.

One more try for him. "What about sex?"

"Now you see it, now you—still sort of see it if you half-squint in the right direction."

"Too difficult. I'm into rot these days."

"You remind me of my ex." She blows another smoke ring, or would if her cigarette hadn't recently drowned in his drink. "If you can't snipe at your husband, whom can you snipe at?"

He purses his lips. "Tell me one secret thing."

"I put my feet on the table just to irritate my mother, though she died five years ago. I'm often homesick for homes I never knew."

"That's two."

"So it is. How about advice? Want some?"

"Like what?"

"Never provide an alibi for a crime you haven't yet committed. Now maybe you should leave."

He ponders this for a moment; thinks about what any conversation will be like without her. He can say nothing. After a pause as patchy as a quilt, he covers up with five words: "I think I love you."

And that ruins everything.

# III

# Ismene

Lemon Grief was a chubby bulimic who hung on to her angry adolescence well into her twenties, then buckled down to write. *If you never met your father's second wife,* she wrote in her journal, *does she still qualify as a stepmother?* Under a heading called "Grief's Reviews," she typed, "*Heaven's Gate* wasn't just a rotten movie—it didn't even suck the way I thought it would." And: "Harry Potter left me utterly bereft."

Her mother let her stay in her old room, though she occasionally muttered, "Sometimes two is one too many." Because of a nasty accident some years back, Mrs. Grief got nauseated whenever she had sex or went on a plane trip, two incidents that occurred roughly every five years. Lemon's father had decamped one afternoon after seeing Christ in the San Diego harbor, lightly jogging over the bay. On Lemon's birthdays, he sent inspirational greeting cards, which she stuck under her bed with the dust mice.

Then Lemon met Dale, a walking basket case, not a writer, thank God, just a café waiter, but thoughtful and observant in a way she wasn't. They began talking on a line for Celine Dion tickets. "Look," he told her on their first date, a frosty night in December, "only seven reindeer in those rooftop Christmas decorations. I wonder who got cut out, and why?" That impressed her, and their dual attempts to be eloquent to each other ended in a tri-syllabic kiss.

On their second evening together, she told him her idea for a novel, *Just for Looks*, about a girl who literally cuts off her nose to spite her face. "Not bad," he told her, "but it doesn't have enough ugly." She wasn't offended because she was already half in love with him. They brainstormed together, coming up with a major slashing scene.

Mrs. Grief waited up for Lemon till she came home at two a.m. The smell of unadventurous cooking still permeated the kitchen. "I once went out with a talker like that," she told her daughter, after hearing a description of Dale, "the kind of attentive listener you tell your whole life story to, thinking he's telling you his." She frowned at the stove. "Be careful."

But Dale was also in love—with Lemon's brains and her bullet-shaped beauty. When they decided it was serious, Lemon took him to visit her father in La Jolla, where they met his second wife, a.k.a. stepmother, Penny. She was young, with a bust broad enough to support all kinds of conclusions.

Lemon's father offered Dale some whiskey aged in oak till it was senile. Over dinner, Penny took a closer look at Lemon's lemony outfit and remarked, "That's a color you might eat but shouldn't ever wear." Mr. Grief started to argue with his wife, but Lemon embarked on a coughing fit.

Dale contributed: "'Everything's fair in love and war' really means nothing's fair in either." For the rest of dinner, you could hear the sound of punches being pulled.

When they got back to Dale's place, they figured it was time. They were quick; they were expeditious. For inspiration, he stared at the dark V of her loins. "You're a clean animal," he told her afterwards. "I like both the clean and the animal part."

What Lemon wrote in her journal that night remains unknown.

Soon Lemon was pregnant but told no one. "You know," remarked her mother, à propos of absolutely nothing, "I think Dale may be related to you."

"Yes, I was adopted," Dale told Lemon at the café where he worked. "What of it?"

DNA samples surreptitiously collected by Lemon showed they were alike as a near perfect simile. And Dale wrote, too, as it turned out—he just didn't talk about it. When pressed, he provided the titles of two poems he'd been working on: "Retrograde Love" and "The Thinking Man's Penis."

Lemon felt betrayed, but by whom? "All right," she told Dale, after getting him mostly horizontal, "here's the story." And she told him.

Dale cursed her father. "Son of a bitch has connections I didn't even know existed."

"My mother, actually."

All Dale could do was spread his hands in surrender. "All right, I'll let you be." Pause. "What do you want to be?"

Lemon covered her belly with her hands. "Unpregnant."

"That can be arranged." Dale stood unsteadily. "This isn't a Greek tragedy. But are you man enough to be my wife?"

Lemon kissed him harder than necessary. They got hitched, and lived carefully ever after. *There's a lot more to life than nice*, Lemon wrote in the third draft of her novel. *We all contribute to the general stink.* Dale looked over her shoulder and changed a word.

# Food for Thought

"I guess eating yourself technically *is* cannibalism," remarked Doctor Wilding, "but other issues are involved here."

"Like what?" Kristin had her arm outstretched, and you could see the cut marks below her elbow. Every lunch hour, she'd retreat to the bathroom, lock herself in a stall, and carve herself a new insignia. Sometimes she was quite artistic. The latest incision was floral and still oozy with blood.

"Well, self-infliction of harm." Doctor Wilding tried to look away from Kristin's arm, so bare and beautiful and scarred, but that was hard to do. The students didn't like him at all, yet somehow he needed their presence to make him feel alive.

"That's no one else's business!" Kristin was a firm believer in *Our Bodies, Our Selves*, a volume she'd stolen from her mother's bottom bookshelf when she started menstruating three years ago.

"Uh-huh, I mean no." Doctor Wilding looked toward the rear of the room, where two backwards baseball cap types were sharing some substance and snorting it. In a moment, their faces assumed the lineaments of gratified desire. But Wilding wasn't the kind of teacher who suffered boors gladly. "Fletcher—yes, you—what do you think?"

Fletcher assumed a forty-five-degree angle imitating thought. "Awww...." He scratched his cap. "Could you repeat the question?"

If Wilding had a nickel for every time one of his students had bought time that way, he'd have paid for his '97 Honda Civic by now. One year he'd had a transfer student from Georgia who drawled "Do what now?" to the same effect. Students nowadays were clever: in his own day, there was no dissembling but a simple, revealing "Huh?"

"I *said*, what do you think?" Wilding placed his hands on his hips. "About eating yourself."

The only reason the question had come up was that they'd been studying the customs of certain West African tribes: ancestor worship using bones of the deceased, for instance, or tribal scarring (Kristin had perked up at that). After battle, it was traditional to drink a little blood of the victims, and what happened, asked Richard, the one truly bright presence in the class, if, bloody from battle, you imbibed some of yourself instead?

As a hyper attention deficit disorder case who made his own desk nervous, Richard soon lost interest in his question, but the class pursued it as if after a wapiti on the plains. It was their afternoon diversion in an otherwise arid expanse of social studies and math. Like a bunch of amateur hunters, though, they soon became distracted and lost sight of their original quarry.

"Like drinking your menstrual blood," offered Kristin, still pursuing themes from *Our Bodies, Our Selves*. She picked meditatively at a scab.

"And yet not." Marianne, the one certifiable babe in the room, wrinkled her nose-job nose. Her long legs, revealed up to high thigh in a miniskirt, were crossed elegantly at the ankles. Her breasts, noted Wilding for perhaps the seventeenth time, were almost too perfect, but that bothered him only on certain days.

"What's it matter?" Fletcher reinserted himself into the conversation like a reminder of unfinished business. "I mean, if it's yours."

"Yeah." Morgan, Fletcher's buddy and partner in pharmaceuticals, nodded in support. "Inside, outside, what's the difference?"

"You wanna know?" Hell, it was Carl the gross-out king, who repulsed even Wilding on occasion. He rooted in his left nostril for moment, producing a greenish-gray nodule on the tip of his forefinger. "This is a booger. It *was* inside me. Now it's not." He held it up for the class to admire.

"Shit, man, keep that thing away from me!" Larson, who ran with a gang called the Hebs and probably carried a shiv, still had a squeamish spot for mucus. He backed away as far as his desk-chair would allow.

"Yuck." Marianne turned away, exposing a cerise bra strap.

"And now," pronounced Carl, "I'm gonna eat it."

With a small flourish, he did, smacking his lips afterwards. That seemed to prove something or other, and no one spoke for a moment.

Sensing a pedagogical opportunity, Wilding opened his mouth. He wanted to goad them. "Carl has a point, you know. If it's inside your body"—and here he looked searchingly at Marianne—"it's safe, beyond inspection. Outside, it's, shall we say, problematic."

Marianne scrunched up so that her body was less on display, more inside her camisole top. But then, as if disagreeing with herself, she shook her head lightly and exposed her armpits in a predatory yawn. Meanwhile, Arthur, the one religious nut in the bunch, raised a lily-white hand and volunteered, "The body is a temple."

"So I've heard." Wilding tendeded toward atheism. "But what does that mean?"

"It's bullshit, that's what!" Tammy, the anorexic girl in the front row, either worshiped at a different diocese or obeyed a different god. "The body is, like, so evil, it's disgusting. It has to be purified." She half-patted, half-slapped her no-stomach. "Starved."

Arthur shook his head. "You should let in the holy spirit."

"Or Christ. That's what the wine and wafer are all about." Edward, black-haired and beady-eyed, the one Catholic in this crazy quilt of students, stuck out his chin as if about to receive communion. He fingered his crucifix, that symbol of extreme agony.

"I know what that means." Richard's sapience might one day get him in a lot of trouble. "You mean you're eating Christ's body and drinking his blood."

"Now *that*," said Carl, "probably grosses most people out."

Time to act. Wilding moved toward the blackboard. In crude but effective strokes, he outlined a stick-figure body. "Maybe the body is merely a conveyor. You know, something like 'He who eats of me gains wisdom.'" He chalked the body into parts. It looked oddly like him.

"Huh?" This from Fletcher in back.

"Suppose I say that cannibalism itself is a holy enterprise? Or that the elders in a tribe, once they die, are eaten so that their strength can be passed along to the rest of the group?"

"Huh." Morgan nodded his approval. "S'kinda neat." He nodded again, and this time Fletcher's cap nodded in unison with his.

"Okay, but how's that work?" Richard wrinkled his high brow, trying to visualize it. "I mean, if it's a symbol, sure, but—"

"It's more than a symbol." Edwin made an assuring gesture he'd lifted from a priest. "It's like a miracle or something."

"Sposin' that guy don' wanna be eaten?" Larson always thought in terms of power: who had it, who wanted it.

"He's, like, *dead*." Kristin, having grown tired of picking at herself, was now picking at others.

"Not always." Wilding felt the need to push them, even if it meant improvising. "In some instances, a live body is required to provide...freshness." Did Marianne just lick her lips at this point? Wilding pressed home his teacherly advantage. "This may be slightly taboo, but to eat someone is also slang for...a sexual act."

"We know, we know." Fletcher and Morgan in back.

"Good." Wilding rocked slightly on his heels, wondering about the taste of Marianne below. Her legs were slightly apart. "No taboos in this class, eh?"

"You mean we can do what we want?" Larson was fingering something in his pocket that looked thin and flat.

"Perfect freedom is an illusion," recited Richard from something he'd obviously read to impress others with. He stood up to say this and then for some reason didn't sit down again.

Wilding considered the statement. "True, but we can suspend the laws of propriety here in this classroom." And was that Kristin giving him the eye, as well? Even if these students hated him, he was clearly getting somewhere this afternoon.

"Like what?" Marianne didn't usually speak like this, but now she was half out of her seat, leaning toward him.

"Yeah, like what?" That was Larson, but Wilding ignored him, advancing forward a bit until his crotch was a few feet away from Marianne's face. Confrontation, that was all these kids understood.

He put a finger in his mouth and pretended to chomp on it. "Mmm, this is good."

"What's it taste like?" Carl, of course.

"Well, not like chicken, I can tell you that."

"Can we eat you?" My God, Marianne was actually standing up, showing that she was an inch taller than her teacher.

Wilding smiled broadly. "Well, maybe as an experiment." Her mouth, those lips.

"We all eat each other," announced Tammy, who looked half-starved.

Kristin was biting her fingernail. Three girls all at once made for a heady vision.

"It might even be considered an act of generosity," he prompted, sliding toward them. He was too old and too tenured to mind any consequences. But as the girls advanced on him, was that a shadow of Larson flanking them?

Kristin reached out for Wilding's hand, which he donated to her, as Marianne bent down to take his left leg. Her grip was thrilling, as her nails raked his skin through the thin fabric of his slacks. But then someone pushed an elbow into his back—the flash of a cap: Morgan? Fletcher?—and he went down onto his knees. Now he was staring upward at Carl, who clumsily removed Wilding's glasses, and was that Edward, making some speech about the passion of Christ? Everything had blurred. He felt a tentative bite on his calf, and then someone sunk a row of teeth into his neck. Involuntarily, he pitched forward, but Kristin and Marianne each had a firm hold and steadied him for Larson's knife, coming from the side.

The class bell rang at just that moment, and Wilding thought he was saved, but instead it rang forever and ever. His last idea was that he had taught a rather successful lesson, after all. He had finally gotten through to them.

# Still Hanging

Daddy said he slept on the living room floor because he liked it there, but I knew he wasn't long for our fourth home in five years, not the way those crescent eyes of his would swivel past the furniture and out the window, down the driveway, toward Route 98 and the chug chugging of trucks and beer. Breakfasts around the kitchen table were like a poker session, Daddy hungover but bluffing behind his newspaper, Momma upping the ante with a platter of fried eggs and grits, and the kids ready to fold any minute.

At school, people would tell us where they'd seen our daddy: In a borrowed Cutlass Supreme, barreling down a dirt road with a bottle attached to his right arm. Staggering about the lanes at Kiamie's, bowling gutter balls as often as he scored strikes (he'd been the league champion before he'd been our dad). Or just coming out of Doc's Eat Place at noontime, wiping his hands on those grease-stained overalls, staring down the alley and licking his lips at Sheryl's Live XXX Girls before heading back to his job at the bodyworks. Or not heading back at all.

"Son," he told me in one of his rare in-between moods, halfway between the loose grin and the flinty silence, "you take my advice. Get out when there's still time."

"Where?" I asked him. I angled my head toward the pine-fringed horizon, but he was mostly blocking my view.

"Shit." He turned and spat in a wide arc that boomeranged against the wind. "If I knew, I'd tell you."

He finally lit out when I was twelve, leaving in the middle of the night when he thought everyone was sleeping. He packed most of his clothes in a cardboard suitcase but left his greasy overalls to dangle on the wash line like a headless daddy scarecrow. Weeks later, Momma cut them down with a pinking shears. Six months afterwards, Roy moved in. He was decent, just not sparky—the kind of guy who'd give you a pen set for your birthday. We never saw Daddy again, except in shadows from the basement and a sometime-ghost in the closet. My sister Angie got a job at Beulah's Beauty Supplies, but I stuck out school until I graduated, then left for Chicago. Moved four times in five years while passing through six jobs and lost touch with almost everyone. Now I work the graveyard shift at a printing plant.

When Momma died last month, I got a much-rerouted letter from Roy too late to attend the funeral. The letter also said that he was sifting through her old stuff and found some clothes that might've belonged to my father. I hear Angie lives way to hell-and-gone in Pasadena, but I might swing by.

I want those overalls back.

# With

At age thirty, Daryl knew that his marriage was the best thing that ever happened to him. At age forty, he felt the same about his divorce. Then he started feeling low, a narcissist who grew to loathe looking in the mirror. He met Lydia in a coed bathing facility with two stalls and one bar of soap. Lydia fell asleep in the shower and woke up to find herself clean. "God," she said after realizing how carefully he had looked after her, "you take really safe showers."

But other than that, Daryl was full of whimsy or something like it. He delivered odd bits of information: "You know, the Chinese Han dynasty had cell phone technology, but the emperor suppressed it." He also asked questions: "Who was hotter, Don Juan or Casanova?"

"You and you and you," she told him, hushing his lips with one strong forefinger. "Sin at leisure," she said afterwards; "repent in haste." She concocted other sayings, many about him, such as "It's hard to put your best foot forward when you can't even get it in the door" and "He who does not work can have no vacation." Daryl had been on disability since the Reagan administration. When asked about employment, he claimed he didn't want to increase the amount of pain in this world.

But she was preternaturally alert, sensing when the moment had passed even before it arrived. She never thought what she had with Daryl would last. One day when the sky was the color of paranoia, she was going to break up with him, but she could hear the unrequited slap of the rope against a flagpole. She could suddenly see life from perambulator to wheelchair. And she couldn't do without.

That old what-iffer, sniffing around the dank clouds of our possibilities. That inveterate duo, love and lack.

# Breakfast of Champions

When I was eleven, my father turned into a gorilla. My mother had died a year earlier, and for a while, as if in penance, we subsisted on raw vegetables sprinkled with a lot of pepper, or ripped-up lettuce with a splash of vinegar. My father and I both grew gaunt before we gave up mourning and switched to a diet of takeout Chinese and pizza. The empty white containers, stacked by the kitchen door every week, loomed like some boxy robot. My father's figure slowly ballooned, and we both felt guilty for turning into pigs. Then one Friday he came home with some canisters of whey powder—and soy supplement and dried egg and casein—and clunked them down on the table.

"What's that?" I'd been expecting another cardboard carton installment from Hunan Garden, even though we'd already called them twice that week.

"Dinner." My father rummaged around a floor-level cabinet in search of an old blender that my mom used to make smoothies after her sense of taste had gone off. He hoisted its glass bell onto the counter and sloshed skim milk into it. He scooped powder from three of the jars, pressed down the blender top, and turned the setting to high. A minute later, he poured the sludge into two jelly glasses and slid them onto the table with a bartender's grace. He'd once part-timed at Flannagan's and still had the moves.

"Bottoms up," my father suggested, holding on to his glass as if it might escape from him. The mixture tasted like an oatmeal milkshake with extra gray added. It was what I imagined concrete might be like if someone turned it into a drink. Since I was still a fairly dutiful son in those days, I sipped and sipped until I reached midway, then closed my eyes and chugged the rest.

Saturday morning, when we usually got up late, my father was bustling around downstairs at seven. I had dozed off around two a.m. after rereading *The Martian Chronicles*, but the whine of the blender cut through my sleep. It became an increasingly familiar sound, along with the grunts from indoor calisthenics. The fresh, sweaty odor of self-improvement already hung in the air.

Breakfast was an egg and more of the protein drink, though I was allowed a bowl of Cheerios as a concession to the power of oat bran. After that, we were off to the garage, where my father had purchased a set of free weights and an exercycle. It was 1970, before the fitness craze and its sleek apparatuses. I don't know what he expected from my doughy, unformed body, but he gave me a few tips as we did a few stretches on the concrete floor.

"Build up to the right weight. Always push away from you when lifting. Go for the burn—that's when you know you've had enough."

But my main activity was to spot him as he lay on the coffee table he'd dragged outside. In case he dropped one of the barbells, he explained. I had visions of the sweaty metal bar throttling him and held my hands out awkwardly just in case, though I wouldn't have been able to do much. He'd slid two of the black York weights on either side to build himself an eighty pound barbell and went for ten repetitions, going slower and slower until he gave up on number seven with a sigh like an air brake. Then he took off some weight and began another exercise, consulting a little manual that had come with the weights. After attempts at presses, lifts, curls, raises, squats, and lunges, he rested on the table, head bent, elbows on knees. I spied a thinning spot at the top of his crown that I hadn't noticed before. When he regained his wind, he got on the exercycle, put it on high resistance, and pedaled as if slogging through mud. Halfway through, he asked me to bring out our kitchen transistor radio and tune it to WBLJ, which accompanied him partway with "Stairway to Heaven." After that came calisthenics, including push-ups, sit-ups, and squat thrusts. He went through three rounds of everything, with me participating here and there, before collapsing onto the pavement. He spent the rest of the afternoon recuperating.

The next day, he was stiff all over, hobbling from bed to chair and back again. I didn't feel so great myself, but we kept to our protein shakes, and he and I went through some stretches together. "This'll keep us limber," he argued, and I nodded silently. The truth is, I had nothing else to do in those days. I had no real friends. I read piles of books and brooded a lot, and squat thrusts were at least a break from that. My father wasn't a gregarious type, especially with my mother gone, but now we smiled at each other, partners in pain.

Thus began a routine: early rising and power drinks, weightlifting and aerobic exercise. Once a week, we went for a two-mile run together, the first few times gasping but eventually able to hold a conversation. I didn't do much with the weights but instead got on the exercycle and pedaled cautiously as he went through his curls and lifts. He seemed to like the company.

My father was a lawyer with a lot of hard-luck cases, from welfare issues to wrongful arrest for shoplifting. Over the years, he'd built up a reputation for doing a lot with few resources, but all that got him was more of the same kind of cases. And many of those he represented were surprisingly ungrateful. From time to time he'd talk about a particularly difficult client he'd taken on.

"Lizzie never paid me. Her ex stopped sending alimony checks when he found out she was seeing other men for, uh, money." He reached down for two thirty-pound barbells to curl. I pretended I understood even when I didn't. Conversation was scarce in our household of two, and this would encourage him to continue. I listened to the story of the man dropped from the welfare rolls after he was found to own two businesses, and I nodded when my father talked about a sex offender who jumped bail. My mother, who'd worked part-time as a teacher for learning-disabled students, had nodded at him in the same way.

I felt the chiding shadow of her at home, where we we'd let the rooms go to hell, each in its own way. Sticky cabinets licked at me in the kitchen, and dust pools circled the twin sofas in the living room. My bedroom was a time warp of old Disney posters and board games, some from when I was five years old. I'd stopped adding to the accumulation when my mother went to the hospital for the last time. By then, she'd wasted away to ninety pounds. She died of complications from leukemia on Thanksgiving.

Maybe that was why my father was now so intent on moving in the opposite direction. In a few months of unstinting effort, he made a surprising change from a pudgy man in his late thirties to a truly fit-looking guy. Exercise is one of the few areas in life where you get out what you put in, if you're also conscientious about diet. The transformation was subtle at first: his pants seemed looser, his shirts tighter. The exercises grew easier, though he tried to compensate by adding weights and varying the routines. He did take a break from his regimen every Friday night, when he rewarded himself with a giant T-bone steak. I can still see him bent over the hibachi he'd bought, irritably poking the beef with a fork to see if it was done enough. We'd wolf down the meat blood-rare, and he'd give me some of his beer.

"It doesn't get better than this," he'd proclaim, then belch loudly. I nodded, too inexperienced to see pathos for what it was.

After about five months, my father was like a bull pawing the dirt. His chest, the last time he'd measured it, was forty inches, his waist down to thirty-two. He had real biceps, the kind that shape up like a banana when you flex. He started wearing muscle shirts, though they didn't flatter his narrow shoulders. And he started seeing women again.

As with so many aspects of grown-up life, I didn't notice much at first. My father told me he'd be home late one evening, and when he came home at eleven, he was smiling to himself. One morning before he showered, he smelled funny, like a combination of aftershave and perfume. Then one evening he told me he was going out on a date.

At eleven, I wasn't that interested in girls, though I liked a few for how gently they'd treated me after my mother died. When the guys were out playing soccer, I was behind the bushes, reading a beat-up copy of last year's *Guinness Book of World Records*. If a girl had approached me, say, Miki Tanaka, with her curtain of black hair that she shook whenever she grew annoyed, the most she would have gotten out of me was a nervous hello. Sure, I knew about sex, but more as a subject in a book (record for most kisses in an hour: 2,774). I don't know what my father thought I knew, but he probably assumed too much or too little. That was his style.

The first woman he brought home was named Belle. She was nice enough, with a smile somehow bigger than her horsey face, but she didn't have much to say, which, with a guy like my father, meant a lot of patchy silences. She sat with her hands laced in her lap, her smile growing nervous around the edges. I was introduced as the other man in the family, heh heh, and then I went back to reading *The Martian Chronicles*. Belle lasted only a couple of weeks, and I'm not sure who got tired of whom. After that, nothing for a while, and my father filled the gap by swimming laps with me in the local YMCA on Saturdays.

I remember when he introduced me to Marie because she cut him off in mid-sentence and performed the lead-in herself. If she and my father had inhabited a comic strip, her speech balloons would have blocked out everything else in the frames. "I said—" my father would begin, and Marie would interject, "So you say," with a playful nudge in his ribs. She was short but extremely animated, touching people as she spoke. I liked Marie, who one Friday took over our sticky kitchen to cook Beef Stroganoff for us, instead of steak. She cursed prettily in French, and she had an unclipped poodle named Clio that I once saw in the back seat of her Renault. But the strain of listening to all that talk eventually told on my father, who must have initially thought it would fill out the evenings. Their break-up was tempestuous, with Marie striding out the screen door and turning to utter one word: "*Clochard!*"

Judging from my mother, my father's taste in women was for short brunettes. Dorothy was the closest to that type. She sized me up for the creature I was, commenting, "Bookworm, eh?" and offering to play me in Scrabble. She had a sense of order and purpose and one afternoon even managed to clean up our wayward kitchen shelves. She hummed old Broadway tunes from *Guys and Dolls* and *Oklahoma* that I knew only from the cast album records my mother had played. Though she was a few years older than my father, I thought he went well with her, acting much younger in her company and even, after a few glasses of wine, letting her cut his hair. Oddly, he was the one who dumped her, as I found out when I asked one Friday where Dorothy was. My father looked away from the grill, its coals reddening like a burning shame. "Oh, she left," was all he said. But she phoned one evening soon after and talked to me because my father was out that night. I found out that he called it quits after she asked to see some of my mother's old jewelry. "He's quite protective of her, you know."

"I didn't." I worried the phone cord with my finger.

"I think he wants to punish himself. Which means he has it in for both of us."

That should have told me something about the direction my father was going. Yet an eligible man in his late thirties was a hot commodity, especially one in decent shape and with a law career. Anyway, now that I was twelve and legally able to stay home alone, as he told me, some nights he didn't arrive at the house till quite late, and once or twice he didn't come back at all. Instead, there'd be a message on our answering machine, the old tape reedy with use. "Kiddo...it's Dad. Sorry...I missed the bus last night, heh heh. I'll...see you at five-thirty."

A change had come over him. The exercise routine that had given him a chest and biceps had also made him cocky. He installed a floor-length mirror by the foot of the stairs, so that he could see all of himself in various poses. He wore a new suit that fit his broadened pectorals and nipped-in waist. "Lookin' good, huh?" he'd say to me or maybe to himself, as he reached out to punch me playfully in the stomach. He sometimes gave demonstrations of his strength that involved hoisting the living room furniture.

Having succeeded at remaking himself, he started talking dismissively of the clients he used to sympathize with. He called them weak and said they'd failed to help themselves. They didn't present the kind of cases he merited. He couldn't seem to find the women he deserved, either: they were nice enough, and yet.

I'm not sure how he met Kathy, but I do recall her entrance. She shook my hand like a man, with a real bone-crusher. She was wearing a blue ribbed tank top and shorts that emphasized the jut of her shoulders and thighs. She spoke in a raspy contralto, saying, "For sure" and "You got it!" It was nine o'clock on a Saturday night, and the two of them had been drinking something that smelled like the bourbon my father kept in the cupboard. Then he made some comment that annoyed her.

Kathy turned on one heel. "Think you're strong?"

My father wasn't sure how to answer this, but after hesitating a bit too long, he muttered, "Yes."

"Okay, then." She curled her hands as if squeezing the air in front of her. "How about we arm wrestle?"

My father's eyes narrowed, then he grinned uncertainly. "You're on."

They sat down to arm-wrestle on the kitchen table, which my mother had used to correct her students' work. It had a plastic tablecloth with yellow blobs of color that weren't quite flowers. In order to get the right reach, my father and Kathy sat across a corner. I wished fervently that I was elsewhere, but it was too late to disappear. Kathy's big hand fit sideways against my father's like a wedge.

I was asked to start them off. "On your marks, get set, go!" The match began with a grunt from my father as he thrust himself forward, trying to use his whole body as leverage. Kathy was savvier, backing off and pushing my father's pressure sideways. As she did, the top of her hand began topping his at an odd angle, as if her fingers were somehow eating his. He tried to regain balance but was steadily pushed downward. By the time he was around sixty degrees, it was all over. Kathy pushed home her advantage, and that was it. His hand hit the table with a defeated thud. They disengaged and sat staring at each other.

"Best two out of three?" Kathy asked, a bit too sweetly.

Sullenly, my father nodded. This time, when they started, my father fairly flew at her in a move that was probably illegal, and at first he forced her backwards, but soon she reasserted herself. After about ten seconds, it was as if she were bending his hand in a direction that it didn't normally go. Near the end, he looked as if he was pleading silently. When she forced him to the table again, he loudly said nothing.

After a moment, Kathy got up from the table. For a winner, she wasn't gloating too much. "Listen, champ," she clapped my father on the shoulder, "for a guy your size, you're not that bad. But don't mess with a lady." And with that, she left through the back door. She drove off in a yellow Mustang, the thrum of the engine as noisy as if the pavement were a drum.

When I looked toward my father, I almost wished I hadn't. *Disappointed* isn't the right word. It was like something stiff had crumpled inside. But when he caught sight of me, he put on a gruff act. "C'mere, boy," he told me. "Let's have a drink. Or three."

He split a beer between two glasses. "What should we toast?" I asked.

"Your mother. My wife."

When I looked closely at his face, I could see a tear in one eye. I might have commented, except that soon I was crying myself. The beer turned into three beers, and more bourbon for him, and the next morning he didn't go to work and I didn't go to school. The diet supplements went into the trash, and the exercise regimen got dropped like a too-heavy barbell. In the weeks to come, we developed another routine, sitting in the living room armchairs, playing checkers, and watching reruns of shows like *Gilligan's Island*. We even tried a bit of home cooking. I knew it was only temporary, the way our lives would be until someone came to save us or else we somehow rescued ourselves, but for a while it was enough, and we sat in our armchairs as if holding on to what we had.

# The Mater-Morphosis

One morning, Greg Samson found himself transformed into his mother. One moment she was lecturing him for not brushing his teeth—"If I've told you once, I've told you—"

"—a thousand times," he finished, though he was talking to a sullen eight-year-old he recognized as a twin of himself. When the boy shook his head, Greg reached out with one broad, fleshy arm, took the toothbrush from the rack, pried open the poor boy's mouth, and began to brush vigorously. The boy was made to rinse and spit. Then Greg went downstairs to start the laundry. Nearly everything was automatic, as if he were lodged in the cockpit of some vast, maternal machine. Shock at his transformation—he was much higher and heavier, with body parts that rubbed—was tempered by an odd equanimity. He found himself strong and capable, even as his body propelled him back upstairs to see how the boy was doing.

The boy lay splayed on his bed, reading a comic book. It was summer vacation, and he had no place to be. So Greg simply told him to take his shoes off the bed and walked away again. Around eleven o'clock, Greg took him shopping. Before that, he had examined his new body, puzzled most by the hairy slit below his waist, which felt too odd for words.

For some reason, he felt little of the panic he might have. What had happened? How? Would he change back soon? Most important, where had his mother gone? The thought that maybe she had turned into her son made him smile. As Greg patrolled the supermarket aisles with him in tow, he reached over to pat his head.

For lunch, Greg made the boy a tuna fish sandwich. In the afternoon, when he was out playing in the yard, Greg watched some television and began making vague preparations for dinner. Whenever he was at a loss for what to do, he let his body take over. Maybe his mother was still watching him as she always seemed to be. Or telling him what to do, as she so often did. How else to explain the way his hands deftly put together a casserole of chicken and green beans and set it to bake at 375 degrees? Dinner was ready at six-thirty, when his father—or husband—came back home.

The kiss on the lips warmed his cheeks oddly. He found himself repeating what he'd heard his mother say so often: "Hi, honey. How was work?"

His father-husband said little throughout the meal. If the man noticed any difference in his wife, he didn't mention it. But Greg felt strange somehow. The mother in him washed the dishes after dinner and put his previous self to sleep after making him brush his teeth again. Forcing him to act properly made Greg feel both powerful and weary, satisfied and guilty at the same time. Then Greg and the husband-father sat on the couch to watch *Will and Grace*. So this is what his parents did after he was asleep, he thought with some relief.

During a commercial, the husband-father reached out to rub Greg's arm, and Greg liked that. But the rubbing continued upward, to Greg's shoulders and softer parts. A dip down to the breasts caused the strangest feeling. When the man finally got up, he pulled Greg with him, speaking in a low voice that Greg had never heard before. Since he wasn't sure what to do, he allowed his body to act for him.

In the bedroom, he got the surprise of his life.

# Waste

The work's simple and repetitive, pick up the trash, pick up the trash, pick up the goddamn trash. They actually gave me one of those sticks with a metal point at the end, called it a waste-removal unit. A rubberized burlap bag trailing behind me like a monstrous hood I've half thrown off. Up and down the roadside from nine to noon and one to five, with a guy in a dirty white pickup riding by occasionally to see whether I'm doing it. I get everything from Styrofoam cups to road kill. You ever stick a spike through the rotted carcass of a dog? Or an armadillo? At first, the body looks like it's sleeping. That's because armadillos, heavy as they are, jump straight in the air when they're scared, hit the radiator grill *bang* on the nose, and get thrown clear. They just lie there stunned, staring at the sky with their claw-paws in the air. They don't crack open till another vehicle comes by. Then they look like a burst shell casing but with all the blood and guts inside.

That's why they gave me a shovel, too. A few of the local frat boys called me Trash Man for the first week and even tried to run me off the side of the road in their BMW, but I whacked the side of the car with the shovel, and that scared 'em off. A lot of folks are convinced I'm crazy, anyway—have to be to do what I did. Just my luck to get one of those new creative judges, trying to make the punishment fit the crime. Two hundred count 'em, 200, hours of community service, which in my case translated to garbage removal. I've been at it for a week now, and it already seems like forever.

My first day, I saw one of my former co-workers ride by. It must've been over ninety-five degrees, and objects shimmered in the heat like they were underwater. He leaned out the window of his truck—took me a moment to see it was Jerry—and crowed, "Well, if it isn't trash hauling trash!" I flipped him the bird and he just drove off laughing.

I guess it's like in the old days when they'd put some criminal in the stocks and let the townsfolk pick and poke at him. I mean, I'm out there dripping sweat like a human sponge, visible from seventeen directions for anyone to make fun of. Which I suppose is part of the point, along with free trash pickup for the town. But hell, why don't they just parade me up and down with a dunce cap on my head and a placard on my back and get it over with? Was my sin really so bad?

People are touchy about these subjects. Or maybe just about me. Yesterday a little old lady, the shriveled-up kind who'd keel over if she didn't have religion sewn up her spine, was walking the other way down CR 206. When she saw me, she handed me a *Watchtower* tract—which I speared expertly on my stick. Christ, you'd have thought I was spearing *her* in the side, the way she carried on. She didn't leave me alone until I—well, she moved off quick enough, anyway.

I'll bet you have no idea what things some people throw by the roadside. A pocket Bible, a big black brassiere, a dead car battery. I go home at night, collapse on my bed, and stare at the ceiling until the darkness takes over my brain. My nightmares are filled with beer cans, used condoms, and cigarette butts. I wake up with a taste in my mouth as if I'd chewed my dreams.

You with me so far? Good. Because you're probably just the kind of audience who grooves on this kind of story, peering at the blue-collar narrative with a sorry beginning and a sorrier end, with some guy named Earl or Dwayne drinking a lot of beer and feeling sorry for himself. I blame Raymond Carver. You know, there's nothing more real about trailer trash than an accountancy school. No reason why incest and abuse has to beat out the subtler forms of neurosis—except that's your problem, isn't it, and you don't want to read about that.

That's the weird thing: pick up any literary quarterly, if anyone picks them up at all, and what you'll read is a numbing series of Dwayne-hates-Jane stories and she hates him back, or maybe just a man in a rut. Some of the newer stories have nasty sex in them, and the latest wave tries to go multicult, but it's all the same model from a kit.

That's why I decided to give you Trash Man, figuring you'd go for it because it seems authentic. Maybe your half-talent creative writing instructor adjuncting between Click-Clack Community College and Hell taught you to admire the simplicity of character or some such garbage. Me, I like clever, sophisticated fiction, mostly crowded out of the small-press short-story market, which is where I hang out. I won't even bring up the subject of humor.

I thought I'd start a new "can't quit 'em so join 'em" type of thing, and see if you bought it. And don't give me any "write about what you know" crap—you know as well as I do that anything can be faked. Hell, it used to be the definition of fiction.

Tell you what: I'll level with you. I mean, even more than I've done already. If you're still reading. There *is* something real in the opening setup. I *was* sentenced to two hundred hours of community service. You want to know what I did? I was caught dumping trash, a whole carload of it—all the manuscripts that I received as editor of a magazine called *The Maximalist*, jettisoned out the window to smack facedown on the pavement or drift sheet by sheet in the backdraft to settle in the roadside weeds. Pages and pages of broken-up couples, dumb male rage, dead animals, senile relatives, trailer park antics, hokey regionalism, instant insanity, and present-tense limbo sent by all of you who never read a lick of literature but figured what the hell. Toss in all those manila

SASE's and castoff copies of journals like *Cloned Quarterly* and *More Stuff*, and it can spread over a lot of ground. When the cop cruiser flashed its lights at me, I was still feeling righteous and gave him an earful. I decided to represent myself, but it made for an odd case. Maybe the judge was right.

So here I am, picking up your trash.

# IV

# Petty Larceny

The third time Marlene stole my wedding ring, I decided maybe it was time to leave. Sure, she'd taken plenty before: a man's yellow vinyl raincoat, a briefcase monogrammed RBJ, a lot of ashtrays (though neither of us smokes), a creamer from a diner, even a bird's nest that's probably still up in the attic somewhere. At one point she discovered a dollar store in the next town, and from there we got beaded key chains, refrigerator magnets, and palm tree swizzle sticks. She's not a common thief, she insists, but a kleptomaniac. At least, that's the diagnosis the therapist handed down—right before Marlene stole his fountain pen, a fancy Mont Blanc with a gold nib.

I looked up the disease in a psychiatric manual, and the description said that it often stems from emotional deprivation in youth. But Marlene by her own admission had a happy childhood, so what is she compensating for? Maybe it's like the gambler's temptation: something for nothing. She's given up attempting to explain, not that I recall her ever really trying. Her ex-boyfriend Mark did warn me before I married her. "Marlene's nutso," he informed me. "And tell her to give my car keys back."

When I told her this, she just smiled. The point is, she doesn't act crazy, at least not in any other way. She doesn't look like a kleptomaniac, either. She's not an unshaven guy wearing a trench coat lined with pockets, or an old lady with an oddly shaped shopping bag. She's actually rather sweet, with a petite but rounded frame, and elfin features haloed by light brown hair. She also has mischievous eyes that seem to include you in the secret, such as that the hostess has a run in her tights and doesn't know it. But other times the secret hits you in the face: a blue striped necktie hanging from the bathroom towel rack, not the evidence of a one-night stand, as I first thought, but something she took from a men's emporium named Otto.

It's not just shoplifting, though. She operates outside shops, as well. This winter she brought back two traffic cones. I gather she can pickpocket, too, and takes items from bags (like that collapsible umbrella sticking out of someone's purse). I once saw her tease off a scarf that a woman on the subway was wearing, and I would have said something, but I saw only the tail end of that maneuver, and by then it was too late to say anything. The touch of her hand is light but warm, comforting—trustworthy.

Back home, when I confront her about it, she casts her eyes downwards. The one time I tried returning a ring she'd boosted, I just got in trouble. For a while, I simply said to myself, "Living with Marlene is an adventure." But she lost her job as a paralegal after too many small thefts, and now she's got a crappy job as a secretary for an insurance company. I mainly support both of us as a CPA. In fact, like a lot of office workers, I used to engage in a little white-collar crime, a ream of paper here or a box of paper clips there, but no longer.

I'm an organized type, and I compartmentalize my life: work, a drink before dinner, TV, sleep, or time with Marlene, who's quite good at improvising fun. And what I don't know about her episodes won't hurt me, I figured.

The problem began when I started missing some personal items myself: my electric shaver, which I found in the hall closet. Three pairs of trousers are still gone, and she says they're in the laundry, but it's been almost a month. And then my wedding ring, a plain 14K gold band, which admittedly isn't too tight to begin with. She must have eased it off in my sleep. I discovered my loss the next day, and then it materialized on my dresser.

"Is this some kind of statement about our marriage?" I asked her.

At first, she just looked down and said nothing. But when I repeated my question, she swallowed hard and said, "I love you."

"I love you, too," I replied, and left it at that. But then my ring went missing again the week after that, and it didn't reappear for three days, when I spotted it by the sink drain in the kitchen. Now the ring has vanished again, and it has yet to turn up. I'm a methodical man, an accountant, for God's sake, and this kind of disorder is nerve-wracking. If I'd known this about her before we married, I'd have—I don't know what I would have done. And anyway, I did know, sort of.

So I confront her about this latest incident. "Why are you stealing from *me?*" I ask her. "What are you trying to tell me?"

"Nothing," she murmurs, reaching out to clasp my hand. Her fingers caress mine as her other hand strokes my shoulder. "Give me another chance." The hands ends up around my waist, then my thighs, and we hobble-step into the bedroom, where I see that the sheets have been stolen right off the bed, leaving the naked mattress. We slowly flop onto it, her hands reaching, searching, finding.

We make love, and afterwards, spooning dreamily against her, I recall our first date, at an upscale diner with chrome napkin holders and creamers in the shape of cows, which Marlene's sleeve kept brushing up against. She told me that I looked nice in my navy sports jacket and reached across the table to push back a lock of hair from my brow. Her smile, so winsome and bright, slowly grew large enough to include everything, including me.

What I'm saying is, she stole my heart.

# Natasha

"My sweater is broken," said Natasha.

"You mean torn?"

"Maybe." She made a face.

We were seated at one of those pinhead-size tables at the No Name Café, which barely fit two mugs and Natasha's elbows. She was wearing a man's navy blue button-down shirt—mine, in fact—tucked sloppily into a pair of low-cost jeans. No make-up on her high cheekbones, the Tatar angles that some models would covet, only on Natasha the effect was of a louche doll, with Oriental-cut auburn hair. She'd have been taller than me if she hadn't slouched. Now she looked let down or disappointed.

*Crestfallen* was the word I was looking for. She was often that way when she made a stab at the right word but ended up cutting herself. Vulnerable, adorable. I patiently explained the difference between items that can be broken versus materials that rip. Vases and chairs. Paper and fabric. She nodded and made a note in a small spiral-bound pad that she carried in her sack of a purse. She half-frowned as she wrote, the ends of her mouth straight as a pin. Her faces were a specialty: puzzled, her violet eyes turned round; exasperated, nose twitching; or absorbed, when she was poring over a tome with a Cyrillic title like a series of broken columns. I kept trying to get her to read more newspapers, but she said she'd had enough news for this decade.

It was early afternoon, and half the customers were reading books, thick ones, and not all in English. This was not a cell phone and laptop kind of place, with triple skinny lattes. The main event here was still black coffee. The owner, a stocky middle-aged man, looked like a barrel in a turtleneck as he moved from counter to table, nodding sympathetically. He'd come from Romania fifteen years ago and was supportive of the immigrant experience. He let people run up tabs and had been known to float loans. He also encouraged what I'd call a polyglot atmosphere. At almost any time of day, you could sit at the No Name Café and catch four or five different languages from people carrying on what sounded like intelligent arguments.

Natasha was a pretty puzzle. It was never entirely clear where she came from—some Eastern Baltic state like Estonia or Latvia, only whichever one I suggested was never right. Had she been fleeing a dictatorship or an abusive boyfriend? Was she a physical therapist or someone in need of therapy?

What's obvious was that she didn't have her green card, a subject that came up often. She was working as an apartment cleaner, which is how I met her. On the piebald cork bulletin board in the café, she'd tacked up a sign about "making apartment good as news." I'm a professional pedant, which is to say that I'm an English teacher, and I like correcting people. Natasha caught me with a red pen one afternoon, deleting the *s* from "news."

"What do you do?" She stood there with her hands on her hips as if pushing herself upward.

"I—I'm just fixing your sign." I hadn't expected to be caught. "It's, well, it's off a little."

"Off? No, on. On board there."

Natasha's English got better quickly, but at the time it was seriously flawed, sometimes comical. Here was someone I could *do* something with, mold her into something finer. Call me Pygmalion or just an interferer. I explained what "off" meant in this context, and for the first time heard her laugh, a red, throaty sound like joy regurgitated. I went on to show why the expression was "good as new," that *news* was recent information, like what one got from reading the newspaper—"only sometimes the news is old."

That laugh again. "You are native speaker, no?"

"Yes."

"Okay, I trust you, maybe."

"Good." I asked if I could buy her a cup of coffee, and she said probably. In those days, she was tentative about many things: her English, what to eat for lunch, how to pay her rent, her future in America. Perhaps I could help, I implied. She was attractive in an odd way, tall and manly, except for her full breasts, which looked out of place on her square frame. Double chested, as she might have said. She was wearing black jeans and a tattered vest over a T-shirt that read inexplicably, "HERE AND NOW."

Once we were seated and sipping coffee, I asked her what her T-shirt meant.

She shrugged, which called attention to that chest. "I don't know. Someone on street sell it to me, three dollars."

I explained "here and now." She said that here and now in America was stupid. God, it was a thrill talking to someone else who wasn't a part of the system. We started arguing about the U.S. government, though it turned out we weren't really at cross-purposes. Stupid versus moronic, those were our contrasting views. But that led to a question.

"Then why are you here?"

"I hear...America is land of opportunity."

"It can be." I thought of my opportunities and what I had done with them. "If you're willing to work hard."

"I am." She flexed her right arm like a body builder. She looked at me appraisingly, though with a different sort of appraisal than I was giving her. "You want me clean your apartment?"

"How much?"

"Thirty dollars."

I hesitated, not because I couldn't really afford it—only that the apartment was such in such a state, I'd have to straighten up just so she could get to the surfaces. I had mounds of unfolded clothing around the bed, books slanting all over the dining area, and an unsuccessfully disinfected bathroom. I didn't have dishes piled up in the kitchenette sink, but that was only because they were elsewhere—on the counter, under the table, or put back in the cupboard without the benefit of a good scouring. It had been that way for over two years, since the last time I'd made a real effort. I kept meaning to put everything away but figured I should get my life in order first. I pondered that for a moment. I also thought about how nice it would be to have her at my place.

She read my pause as a bargaining ploy.

"Okay." She nodded slowly. "I make it twenty-five. But you help me with English, maybe. Can do?"

"Can do." I'd never heard my language spoken quite this way. I was enchanted and gave her my widest grin. "I'd be happy to."

*

That Thursday morning, I was patrolling my apartment in my underwear, which didn't take long. It was a studio space as big as a bunch of walk-in closets joined together, renting for something just this side of reasonable. In the bed area, I started folding the clothing that looked like a scattering of dead birds, half relatively clean, but ended up cramming most of it into the closet. The rest went into the already stuffed dresser, a three-tiered dwarf that I'd had since high school. The books got stacked in a corner, the dishes put in the sink. I wanted her to think well of me, an American male in his prime. I swabbed here and there a bit with a wet bath towel. It was one of my days off from work, and Natasha had said she'd come at 2:00.

Precisely at 1:53, the outer door sounded from below. Damn. I buzzed her in and stood in my doorway like a sentinel, in a pair of almost-clean jeans and a red polo shirt I'd rescued from one of the mounds. "You're early," I told her as she came up the stairs.

"No, on time. Your clock must be retarded." She had a cardboard box under one arm, which she set down with a thump on the floor. In it were a bulgy bottle of cleaning fluid, a mop head that had suffered a bad haircut, and some rags of rags. She looked around the apartment curiously. She shook her head. "Mess." She pronounced the word like a diagnosis.

Then she got to work. It took her over an hour and a half to clean my small place, with me mostly hanging around and trying to look busy, though all I had to do that day was go food shopping. She dusted with a shredded rag and a strong flick of her wrist. She borrowed my vacuum cleaner and pushed it up and down the throw rug. She mopped the floor and even got under my bed, where a parade of dust mice lived. As she cleaned, I carried on a desultory conversation with her about job possibilities, fixing an error here ("this take time") and an imprecision there ("I correct dirt"). The contrast between what she had and what she wanted, a menial job versus some kind of gig with a band, was poignant. Watching her scour my toilet was a bit embarrassing, but when she bent down, she revealed a sexy crescent of lower back between her jeans and her thin sweater.

She liked me. At least I think she did. She smiled more or less in my direction from time to time. And she *listened*. We talked until she finished, with a flourish of a rag like a military surrender. Then I had an idea. "Look," I said, "I've got some clothes I never wear that would fit you just fine." At first she protested, but I yanked out a yellow shirt and a pair of brown slacks from my dresser and shoved them into her arms. "Go ahead, try them on." I steered her toward the bathroom, and even though she may have suspected a trick, she had a practical streak. She went inside, locked the door with a click, and came out a few minutes later wearing what I'd given her. I'd been right: the fit was good. In fact, she looked a lot better than me in that same outfit. Somehow the shirt had assumed the proportions of a blouse, and the pants clung like a dream.

She turned to look in my bedroom mirror and seemed doubtful. "Looking good?"

I nodded, counting out twenty-five precious dollars into her callused palm. I wanted to prolong the moment but suddenly couldn't think of what to say. All I could come up with was "Same time next month?"

"Sure." She showed her tantalizingly brief smile. "Four weeks okay? Why not?" Then she piled her cast-off clothes into her cleaning box, hoisted the box onto her shoulder, and clomped out of my apartment. From my one window, I watched her cross the street, turn left, and disappear down the block. For a while, I stared at the spot on the sidewalk where I'd last seen her, as if she might reappear any moment.

The next day, I tried calling her, but all I got was her voicemail: "I cannot be reached. Leave one message." I left a few, then gave up. I went back to the No Name Café several times—all right, more than several—but had no luck. In my mind, I talked to her, corrected her funny expressions, and stared into those violet eyes until I saw something stir. But I didn't really see her till four Thursday afternoons later, at precisely two (I'd reset my clock). Once again, I was off from work. This time, she had a larger array of cleaning implements, including some brushes and a real mop. She was wearing my shirt and pants, which touched me but also was slightly annoying: they'd probably get ruined that way. In any event, I complimented her on her appearance, and she nodded uncertainly. That lack of confidence, so seductive in certain women! Once again, as she went from bed to sink, we talked—at first about my job, but I turned the subject back to her work. At this point, she had ten apartments to clean, "each many bigger than you."

I gently corrected her, and then she said something about making all ends meet, so I set her straight on that expression, and we went back and forth like that for the single hour it took her. Maybe the first cleaning had cleared the way for this one, or else she'd grown more efficient. The sway of her breasts when she attacked the floor inspired me to write a poem I never finished. At the end of her stint, I presented her with another cast-off shirt, which she accepted without much comment. Her other clients probably paid her more. She left that afternoon, humming an odd but catchy tune, with occasional lyrics I couldn't understand. The music stayed in my head for days.

That Tuesday, when I had a free afternoon, I happened by the No Name Café, where I finally got lucky. I found her sitting in the back and frowning over a notebook. That was the day she claimed her sweater was broken. I gave her a little talk on the right verb for the job, from *ripping* and *tearing* to *breaking* and *crumbling*, and she nodded, but she still wanted to show me her sweater. She extracted it from her bag, neatly rolled up to avoid creasing. She was right: the zipper was broken, missing two teeth near the bottom.

When I explained the difference to her, she laughed triumphantly and poked me in the ribs. "Broken like I said." She held out the two edges of the zipper. "But can you fix?"

"Sorry, no can do." I sighed. "There are a lot of things I can't fix."

We sat and talked for a while longer, with her asking most of the questions—about America, about me. She asked about the gap between the rich and the poor in this country. She wanted to know about my job and why I was free on certain weekday afternoons. I mumbled something about a flexible schedule and night classes. When she excused herself to use the bathroom, I stole a look at her notebook. It looked like half journal, half English lesson, though a lot of it was written in a language that looked like Russian. One word was underlined twice, alongside a tiny doodle of someone in bed. In one place, the English phrase "half-cooked thought" was crossed out and replaced by "half-baked idea." What odd mistakes. Why wasn't she focusing more on basics?—yet how diligent she was. My hardworking woman. I tried to recall the last time I'd been that way about something, but couldn't.

*

Eight weeks passed. Her English was definitely improving. Never mind how many times I tried to contact her in between cleaning sessions. Once I asked her why she didn't return calls. She said she'd switched phones, but the new number was equally unresponsive. This particular Thursday, she either cleaned faster or more dexterously because she cut her hour-record by five minutes. Somehow she looked bigger, or maybe I'd just shrunk a bit into myself. She'd also prepared some questions, rather than just talk and have me correct her. Where was a bank friendly to low balances ["good for small change"]? How much was a cheap car? Some I couldn't answer, like the average American income or the latest U.S. weaponry. And all this time she was mopping and dusting like a six-armed goddess, with me retreating so as not to be cut down by the windmill. She was wearing a scoop-necked sleeveless blouse (maybe other clients also gave her clothes), and whenever she reached for something, I could see her armpits, with damp little tufts of auburn hair. I wanted to fit into those arms, nuzzle against that broad, forgiving bosom, teach her what to do with me.

At the end of the job, she stood up straight. "I work hardly, no?"

That puzzled me for a moment, but then I had to laugh. "You mean, 'I work hard.'"

Her face collapsed—or broke, or ripped. She picked up the broom and whacked her thigh. "I never get it right!"

"Hey, you're learning." I laid my hand on her solid shoulder and patted her a few times. She let me do that until the pats turned into an attempt at a caress, at which point she shrugged me off, and I ended up stroking the broom.

"Sorry," I muttered.

"Is okay. I understand." She slapped *my* shoulder as if returning a kindness. "But I'm—what? Not buying right now." She pinched my cheek and started to pack up.

I can't describe how I felt. All right, I'll describe it. Bereft. Speechless. After she left, I stared hard at the last place she'd cleaned, the kitchenette sink, and recalled how she looked, the line of force extending from her back through her outstretched hand. When I half-closed my eyes, I could still see her there. I didn't move for almost half an hour, just communing with her cleaning spirit. Then I made myself either a late lunch or an early dinner, which is to say that I popped a frozen mini-pizza into the microwave. I checked my e-mail to see whether anyone had contacted me, but all I saw were three spam messages advertising prescription drugs. For a while, I surfed the web, then read a chapter from a P. D. James mystery I'd taken out from the public library. I was in bed by ten, staring at the ceiling that always looks as if someone had thrown cottage cheese at it. At least now the floor and the surrounding surfaces were clean.

I suffered but survived. I missed some work but missed Natasha a lot more. Surprisingly, or maybe not so much, she came back next time as scheduled. Before starting to clean, she peeled off her long-sleeved shirt to reveal a cerise tank top. I was in bed, still looking for a reason to get up. I'd arisen only to buzz her in but then slid under the covers again after unlocking the door. Now she clapped her hands once. "Out," she commanded. "You know what time it is?"

I half-nodded.

She flexed her arms, showing the wires under her skin, and looked hard at me. "So?"

"So what?"

"So you must get out."

I yawned. "You mean 'get up.'"

"Yes, this you must do."

I stretched in a Y. "Make me."

Without a pause, she marched to the bed and yanked at my feet. I laughed, but that just made her angry. Clamping her arms around me, she heaved upward. Her breasts mashed against my chest, our lips almost matching, her breath smelling vaguely of cinnamon. I wanted to pull her horizontal, but she was too strong.

She hauled me off the bed—or out of it—and sat me on the floor. I was in my underwear as she loomed over me. "Now you must get up and out. So I can clean."

What else could I do? Declare my infatuation? I dressed quickly and left the apartment, unsure where I was headed. I ended up at the No Name Café, nursing a black pool of coffee and looking around, maybe for another someone like Natasha, only of course there wasn't one. Instead, a dyspeptic-looking man with a cliff of a forehead was taking furious notes on a yellow legal pad as he crowded one of the tables all by himself. The other customers at this hour were mostly take-out: places to be, jobs to do.

After almost an hour away, I slunk back home. Natasha was just scouring the kitchenette sink, the final step of her routine. So much activity in such a small space. Natasha's face was flushed the color of a peach from her exertions. I apologized profusely for my laziness, as I put it. She seemed to accept what I said. Yet as I paid her, I felt the same thrill as always: this active, sensual woman was working for *me*. I was about to usher her out when I thought of something. "Hey, what about your English lesson?"

"Oh, that." She shook her head. "Is—it's okay. Maybe some other time." She came forward to hug me, crushingly hard, letting go almost as soon as she squeezed. Then she hoisted her large cleaning rucksack onto her shoulders and exited my place. This time when I watched her leave the building, she went straight instead of turning, and if I wasn't imagining it, walked with a more purposeful step. She didn't look back to see the mock wave I gave her.

I turned back to my empty room. This time, a fine edge of dust flanked the carpet, and the surfaces didn't look as spotless as after her last visit. I began to look around like a jealous lover. When I went over to my desk area, really more of a shelf, I saw that some of my books and papers had been disarranged. Nothing was missing, as far as I could see. Maybe she always shuffled things around to clean underneath, but it rattled me.

On top and to the left was a battered Roget's thesaurus and a Random House unabridged dictionary, second edition. Beside the books rested a sheaf of papers sort of sorted into IN, OUT, and LIMBO. The IN stack contained forms I should have filled out a while ago, including some insurance company follow-ups, slightly beside the point because my coverage had expired a few years ago. Overlapping those were some teaching materials I had yet to go through, something to do with if-then sentences and the proper use of the subjunctive. But many of my ESL students could barely get the hang of *would*, let alone its proper syntactical use. LIMBO was a far thicker pile: anything I didn't want to deal with, from my 2006 tax return to a long letter from my mother, once enclosing the latest check (long cashed) and asking me to come home for Christmas. The OUT stack was nonexistent.

Or it usually was. Resting like a feather in an empty nest was a scrap of paper with Natasha's boxy, Eastern European script. I picked it up and read it once, twice.

"YOU I PITY," she'd written, in pale purple ink like the dried blood of some rare animal. I crumpled it up and tossed it toward the wastebasket, but missed, and let it sit there on the carpet for someone else to clean it up. There was no work for me that week— none of the regulars was sick—so I mostly stayed in the apartment and puttered.

I waited a long time. The days passed like a pack of worn-out cards shuffled and re-dealt without much skill. Natasha didn't come back next month, though I was there punctually at two on Thursday afternoon. I had prepared a short speech, explaining why I did what I do, and where I intended to be in five years' time. When by three-thirty no one had come by, I delivered my speech to the far wall, where a copy of a Hopper painting hung crookedly. It's the one called *Nighthawks*, where a trio of diner patrons wait for who knows what.

That evening, I decided to search for Natasha at the No Name Café, but the place was full of no-Natasha. Her cleaning service sign had been taken down, leaving a pale patch. I don't know what came over me, but I started to sniffle and then to weep, and soon I had to leave.

I thought of writing her but never got around to it. And even if I had, where would I have sent it? The latest phone number for her cleaning service was—out of service. Over the next few months, my apartment grew more and more disordered. I lost my job. By April, I'd heard from someone at the café that Natasha had joined a band in New York, moved to Seattle, gone back to wherever she'd come from, or d) none of the above. It made me feel lost, and I'm still recovering. I could have helped her, I'm sure of it.

I dream of her some nights, whisking her broom around my prone body as if she were purging me of dust. I want to grab hold of her and say, "Sweep me into your arms, okay?"

She expands till she bumps against my ceiling, pushing at the ragged contours of my dream. She tilts her head back, and I can see a word emerging from between those taut lips. "Nokay," she replies.

# Going Nowhere

Pat's a better man than I am, even though she's biologically female. I like to think I taught her everything she knows—and a few things she didn't. When I first met her, she was crying, "Free me, free me!" though she didn't look bound in the least. Bobbling breasts like milk in motion. I informed her I had the right to get angry at every woman who didn't choose me. She had furry tastes, is all I can say.

A little filth is cleansing, she told me later.

I'd considered myself a kid for years, but now I'd reached that dangerous age: thirty-five. This girlfriend of yours, my friend Al prodded eventually, what's she doing besides being twenty-two?

She dangled in front of me the promise of mayhem. She'd suck on a cherry popsicle Christ, frozen on two sticks like a crucifix but melting quickly under that thrusting tongue of hers. Sure, we can get hitched, I finally told her when she was taking a shower. Which parts of me do you want married? It's not one of those life-decisions like chicken or fish. But saying that was like shooting myself in the foot and putting it in my mouth. She did something to me that still twinges in damp weather. She made me say, "I love you."

She wore a wedding dress that stuck out in several directions, and we had a no-bitch clause in the nuptial contract. Let's just say that she's Ms. Pull and I'm Mr. Push.

The trick of marriage isn't doing it once but again and again. It takes more effort every year. I have nothing to add, only subtract. Some nights we leave the dog inside to babysit the kids. "And they lived happily ever after" is back in the days when it was easier to tell a story. A little dullness is probably good for the soul. But I'd be lying if I said I was telling the truth.

# Accommodations

"It's your turn to take Henry shopping," I tell my wife when she finally gets home, and she gives me a dirty look.

"But I just got back from work." Jean steps out of her black pumps with a sensual lift and drops her briefcase by the door. She's a large woman with a scowl, wearing a black tailored suit. "It's not as if I've been painting my nails." She works for a software firm called Data.com and regularly arrives on our doorstep at seven in the evening or later. Now it's seven-thirty, and I've been in most of the day. Apart from an hour when Henry watched *Sesame Street* and an afternoon nap, I've had almost no time to myself. Last year, I quit my job at GraphiCo to be a freelance web designer—but really to spend more time with our adorable, precocious, maddening son, who's approaching four. He's a cross between a cherub and a gnome. His gray blue eyes pierce through everything.

"All right," I say, noticing the puffy circles under her eyes. She looks like an executive raccoon. "Why don't you have a glass of wine, and *I'll* take Henry to the supermarket?"

The offer strikes her like a blow to the chest. "No—that's not right. You've had him all day. I need to run some other errands, anyway."

Is that guilt speaking, or just contrariety? I press my home-advantage. "But you've put in a lot of hours today. I can see it in your eyes. Look, there's an open bottle of Beaujolais in the fridge. Why not just get yourself a glass and—"

"What's the matter with my eyes?" She swivels toward the hall mirror, fingering her crow's feet. She's not the thirty-two-year-old woman I fell in love with, but then, I'm not the athletically trim artist she married. That was seven years ago, and, as my father used to say, with a *whoosh* of his hands, there's been a lot of water under the dam since then. Or is it over the dam?

"Nothing's the matter. You just look—tired, that's all." And fed up with the situation here, like me. "Get some rest. I didn't get much done today, but I can put in a couple of hours after Henry goes to sleep. Maybe if you just tuck him in...."

"No, I could use a break. I mean, I haven't seen him all day." The point is that she's been working, but both of us secretly enjoy work, which makes us feel clean and productive, the opposite from the way you feel after staying home to play seven games in a row of Chutes and Ladders. Of course, Henry is probably listening to all of this, which should give us pause. Jean rounds the corner into our combination den-TV area-playroom. "Hen-*ry*? How are you, sweetie?"

Henry doesn't answer. He's sitting in what I call the uneasy chair next to the sofa, wearing mini-cargo shorts and a Disney shirt, slowly thumbing through a picture book. Ever since we taught him the alphabet last month, he's been learning to put the letters together. "What does *t* plus *h* make?" we ask rhetorically. "That's right, *thhh*"—with a little spray of saliva that he ducks. And the next time, by God, he's got it down. No one can say Henry's not a bright kid. He's already reached the stage where he can stumble through *Hop on Pop*. An absorbed child is a less demanding one. That would give me more time to read, too, an activity I miss sorely.

But Jean hasn't seen him all day, having wisely left before we got up. And now she's going to make up for it—watch this:

"*There* you are, Henry! Give Mommy a hug!"

A bear-cub hug and a smack on the cheek.

"What are you reading, hmm?"

"A book."

188 | David Galef

"I can see that." She cranes her head like an architect's lamp. "Which book?"

"This book." He points.

"All right. I'm sure it's a good one."

"How do *you* know?"

As old-time authors say, we shall draw a veil over the rest of the exchange. Suffice to say that Henry gets yanked off to the local Pathmark with Jean's promise to let him read more in the shopping cart. Henry makes on odd sound when he's indignant, and only after the final squawk dopplers down the driveway do I take a full breath. I lie down on the couch and shut my eyes for a minute or two.

In the dark, I could be a thousand miles from here. On a beach underneath a coconut palm or in the middle of a deserted park. But this time, under heavy-lidded darkness, I'm in the center of a room with no windows, binding something—no, someone—to the floor. The body is wet and naked, deliciously vulnerable. The rope I use is sticky, as if soaked in molasses, and practically attaches to itself. But the figure below, when I finish tightening the cord, turns into mist.

The sound of the back door banging shut wakes me: the rest of my family, returned from their shopping expedition. Henry likes to announce every item purchased, and that's what issues from the kitchen: "Eggs, bread, my milk, Mommy's coffee milk, pisghetti...."

One day he'll get that last word right. Meanwhile, I cherish it. I open my eyes, a bad taste lingering in my mind. I wander in. "Pasta for dinner?" Henry eats almost nothing else, and no sauce, either. "I'll boil some water."

"Oh...I thought we could have a nice salad." Jean's hand is at her mouth, presumably covering but actually advertising her disappointment.

"Sure, okay." I let a load of tiredness flatten my tone. "Did you buy any lettuce?"

"Mesclun mix." Which she knows I think tastes like leaves. I move over to the sink in our cheerful yellow kitchen. "Want onion in that salad?"

"We don't have to eat salad tonight—"

"That's *okay*." I happen to make good salads, and none of that store-bought creamy dreamy dressing, either. That's not the point.

"But if you don't feel like it...."

I let her trail a bit too long before I tell her it's all right. "What about Henry?"

We do this a lot as part of the accommodation game: give in as a weapon, making sure the other person knows how much of a concession you're making. Then deploy Henry as a wedge. Years ago, in some old anthropology textbook, I read about the Potlatch society, where the aim is to give a bigger gift than the one you receive, back and forth to the point where you might lose your home. Generosity as aggression, impoverishing you while bestowing upon others something they don't really want. Our version of the game applies guilt so masterfully that the mere offer of a favor is denied, but you get points just for offering. And invoking our child just twists the knife.

So of course Jean caves in and in a small, tight voice says that pasta will be just fine. But by that time I already have the salad spinner out. Score! To cap my victory, I also thunk our pasta pot onto the front burner, for Henry's sake, naturally.

Henry, who's been folding the shopping bags into odd triangular shapes on the linoleum, looks owlishly at us but says nothing. You could cut the guilt with a trowel. We all end up moodily picking at our dinner, leaving varying amounts of pasta and salad on our plates. Then Henry goes back to folding his bags, which look like headless birds. Of such moments are our days made.

The next morning, Jean is off again at seven—not so fast, Jean! Before she leaves, I make sure she knows what a wreck my day is going to be, without someone to come spell me in the afternoon. Jean thinks most daycare centers are where Bad Stuff Happens, so we make do with an occasional babysitter. Today it'll be nothing but the Henry Show. But as a minor gambit in the accommodation game, I make Jean a breakfast of toast and eggs that she doesn't really want and suggest I drive her to the station, an offer she declines.

You really shouldn't, and I mean that.

"Bye bye bye bye bye!" Henry waves at her from the kitchen window like a man on an ocean cruise seeing land for the last time in a month. But I feel a bit asea, too, with no landmarks or schedule. My web designer job affords enormous flexibility—I can type nude at three a.m. if I want—but I miss colleagues, takeout coffee, a change of air. Instead, I hunker down in front of my computer and respond to whatever the client wants, which is, most recently, flying pigs to advertise a mail-order barbecue business, and a kitchen supply company called *Let's Get Cookin'*! that wants more hot buttons than it knows what to do with.

It's amazing how uncreative most people are. "That's what we pay people like you for," laughs Jean, though Data.Com is far too large to be working with me. But one afternoon last week, Henry approached my workstation and asked why I didn't make the red circles a little bigger and farther down. He *knows* things. And he has a flair for proportion and display.

On the other hand, our days tend to be shapeless unless I inject some order. I'll get some work done after lunch, when Henry is napping, and later I'll plunk him in front of the TV. He lives in a cartoon world where boy-faced dogs whack each other on the head with oversized mallets.

List of activities we can do with Henry, who's bright but afflicted with what neither of his parents wants to call ADD: start a game, any game, for at least five minutes before someone has to go to the bathroom or asks for a snack or simply up-ends the board; take him on errands, anything from a supermarket run to a host of pick-ups and drop-offs—hardware store, dry cleaner's, bookstore—but then there's the matter of monitoring him, since one second you're buying grapes, and the next moment he's in the parking lot, beckoning to a Chevy Suburban; or watch television with him, which isn't so bad, except that the show is probably kiddy-krap, and you can feel it impressing its mindless values on your brain until it's time for a commercial hawking schlock.

At mid-morning, we trudge seven blocks to Ridgeway Park, whose playground features a lot of odd colors and shapes, including a vaginal crawl space and giant rings that look like IUD's. I share bench-space with stay-at-home moms and nannies and one househusband named Dwight, who's all pale white angles stuffed into overalls. Most of the adults run the gamut between constant monitoring and reading the newspaper while listening to an iPod, oblivious to whatever's happening on the swings. I fall somewhere in between, bringing a book but rarely finishing a chapter. I look away mainly to check out some particularly foxy mom, like the twenty-something redhead whose breasts jut forth from a soft cotton sweater and could fit so comfortably in the palms of my hands.

The day is sunny but cold, like the smile on a bureaucrat's face. I'm reading an old James Bond novel that I found at a rummage sale: *From Russia with Love*. It's dated but has its moments, like the descriptions of the Russian officer Rosa Klebb during interrogations, which might be droll if they weren't so horrifying. Henry's amusing in his own way, though an attention-hog like all small children. "Look, Daddy, I'm pumping by myself! Look at me now—I'm halfway to the bar!" I haven't yet found a way to play the accommodation game with him, probably because he doesn't experience remorse the way adults do.

"Do you want a nice push?"

"That's okay."

"Here, just a small shove."

"No!"

"One, two three...."

After ten minutes on the swings and a desultory game of tag with two other kids, Henry switches to the slide, a pink plastic corkscrew that starts in a cockpit and ends in a blue rubberoid mat. I've gone back to my novel. Except for the newspaper, these days I read mainly for escape, but where am I running to? I let my gaze wander to a young mother by a doublewide stroller who's got a bottom shaped like a plum. When I next look up to see Henry, an older girl on the slide—six, seven?—is straddling him. He's in the open-coffin posture that some kids use to go down slides, only he can't move because she's—yes, she is—she's sitting on him! He can't even raise his arms to defend himself because her big knees press down on him, and now she's reaching forward to poke him, and he protests in an odd staccato I haven't heard from him before.

I crane my neck to see better. Is he in pain? Should I intervene? I'm about to yell something when she releases her hold, and Henry slides under her legs with a whoosh. The scene isn't repeated, and soon after the girl goes to play on the jungle gym. But I replay it in slow motion as we walk home. When Jean gets back, I mix her a stiff drink, and that night after Henry's asleep, we have some fun on our own. It's my idea to turn the bed into a slide. Like most big women, Jean's a bit self-conscious, but she likes being on top because the angle's better for her. Her hefty forearms bridge me as she pumps up and down, and I reach around her broad back to hold on for all I'm worth.

Only sometimes we take a lot longer, and the sex is far more fraught. Jean likes me to go down on her but is slightly ashamed to ask for it. I like squeezing against breasts, between thighs, and under buttocks, so we pretend it's foreplay gotten slightly out of hand. We accommodate each other without even asking, which is the opposite of our guilt-infliction and nudging during normal hours.

Cut to Saturday, and Jean's tennis match with three women friends, all in tennis whites that reach to mid-thigh. They toss that poor ball overhead with a contemptuous flick of their wrist and smash it over the net, then whack it back. I can think of all sorts of reasons not to be that ball, but as I sit on the sidelines with Henry, who's thumbing through a Curious George book, I can't take my eyes off those brutal women and their forehand smashes. Forty-love, game.

After the match, I offer to watch Henry for another couple of hours so that Jean can have a drink with the girls. I say this in front of the three other women for maximum effect.

Of course, Jean protests. "No, you've had him all morning."

"That's all right. Just give us a ride back home."

"Wow, what a hero!" This from Jean's tennis partner, a woman named Barbara with a bosom like a battering ram.

Jean pouts but accepts, and I get pleasure from both putting myself out and putting her out at the same time.

But Jean doesn't come back till three in the afternoon, and I park Henry in front of the TV so that I can take a nap on the couch. I shut my eyes ands ears against Bugs Bunny, and I'm back to the windowless room, now lit by some insect-like glow. It's as if I'm picking up where I left off from the previous dream. The binding is complete, the body on the floor almost mummified in cord, though open at certain key areas: the groin, the rectum, the mouth. The figure is small and defenseless, or the room has widened. A woman enters and does something to the body with her nubbin-shaved armpits that leaves it breathless.

What's happening to me? I can't talk about something like this with Jean. Instead, I snipe at her, play the accommodation game the very next evening, offering to be the one who shuts off the light, then getting up in the middle of the night to see what Henry wants—"No, no, that's all right. You have to go to work early to-morrow"—though I can't figure out what the matter is. His room is down the hall, and he's been calling out for a minute. He's a peevish lump under the miniature Amish quilt that Jean bought for him on a trip to Pennsylvania.

"What took you so long?"

"I was asleep." I make sure he can see me yawn.

"Oh." He considers this information. "Well, you're awake now."

"Sort of. What seems to be the problem?" I lay a heavy hand on the bedside, waiting for an explanation.

He squinches his eyes. "Bad dreams."

Before I can pursue this, Jean appears in the doorway, maternal guilt having levitated her out of bed. "Okay, why don't you take over?" I mutter, and stumble back to the parental chamber. Jean comes back in five minutes later, her nightgown slightly disheveled.

"What happened?"

"Night-time frights. He said his closet looks like an evil playground." She settles onto her side, her weight slanting the mattress. "So I shut that door."

"Oh." I turn on my right side and try to block out everything, or else I'll start worrying about playgrounds, too. My last thought before I drift off is this: what if dreams are genetically passed on? My father never complained about sleeping badly, but in his later years he had a fondness for Nembutal. He never hit me but rather ignored me. My mother was what they used to call a homemaker, a role I seem to have taken on. And where did I get my kinks?

The next morning, we're all cranky from lack of sleep, the grit in all family beds. Like a slow-motion film, we push through breakfast. I'm pouring cereal for Henry when I look over at Jean and suddenly can't stand her morning granola, her "I'M THE BOSS!" coffee mug that I had Henry pick out for Mother's Day. But instead of lashing out, I reach over to massage her tired shoulders. I move up to her neck and thumb the hollows just below the base of the skull, where all the tension starts. She tells me I don't have to do that, and I say I know. It feels good, like a bottom directing from below. Henry watches curiously, then pushes over Mommy's coffee.

"Damn it, all over my blouse!"

"Jean, he didn't mean it." Translation: You're a bad mother.

"I know that." She dabs futilely at the milky-brown stain just above her waist. "It's just—"

"I'm sorry, Mommy." Henry looks stricken. "It was a—an *accident*."

Like hell it was. But it's time to accommodate everyone. "Henry, that was good of you to apologize. Jean, why don't you rush upstairs and change? I'll make another cup of coffee and put it in your travel mug."

"That's okay, you don't have to do that."

"S'all right."

"But—"

"Just *go*."

I've got the upper hand here. There's not even time to argue. When Jean comes down again, I offer her the coffee mug, sealed and ready to go. But she surprises me, backhanding the mug into the sink. "Fuck you," she tells me, and disappears through the slamming front door before the other shoe can drop. I explain to Henry what "waiting for the other shoe to drop" means.

"You mean something else bad happening."

"Smart boy."

Somehow we get through the day with minimal agitation. When Jean comes home at seven, we simply don't discuss it. That evening, I tongue her till she moans.

I want to hurt her. Instead, we have another quarrel, this one about our arguments, leading to a feeling of powerlessness, and that scene will be repeated again and again, compensated by more wordless acts. I read some Rilke when I was in college, and the one line that stayed with me is "You must change your life." Easy for a poet to say, I think.

Now it's three days later, and nothing's been solved. Here we are, walking toward Ridgeway Park, Henry trudging in that awkward toddler way that will eventually flatten out to adult plodding. Jean's at work. We've been to the park a dozen times in the last two weeks, repeating the same experience like some half-rate magician flipping through a pack of soiled playing cards that are all the same.

I pick up what's left of my James Bond book as if I were engrossed. In fact, I'm reading, eavesdropping, and monitoring Henry all at the same time. Multi tasking, I heard recently on NPR, is really just quick back-and-forth, and it can steal your brain if you're not careful. The woman with the busty sweater is chatting with, of all people, Dwight the misfit. He looks even dorkier than usual, his limbs like a marionette's with tangled strings. And his kid looks the same. What kind of home life can he possibly have, and what's his wife like? I'd like to watch the two of them go at it, but this is territory I can invade only in my imagination. "Not so fast, Mr. Bond."

That prone figure in my dreams, I suddenly realize, is either me or my son.

When I look up a minute later, at first I can't see Henry. He's not on the slide where I last saw him. No, there he is, haloed in the mid-morning sun, halfway up the jungle gym. He's hanging by his thin arms as if waiting for something or someone. From behind comes that girl I recognize from the slide, her thick thighs swallowing the horizontal bar she straddles. She calls out, Henry looks back, she reaches out, and this is where my vision grows hazy. Should I call out? Against the glare, I can see her tickling his left armpit to make him lose half his grip, as he giggles in that pained way that means both "stop" and "don't stop." Then she swings forward and reaches out, and the next I know, he's slipped through her encircling arms to the pummeled sand below.

For a moment, I just stare at the neat little body, paralyzed as if it were me immobilized down there. The limbs are splayed out like a giant starfish or an accident victim. Then he starts bawling, which propels me toward him—"Henry! Henry! Are you all right?" The girl half apologizes, though she doesn't seem to mean it. Henry levers himself up. It turns out that nothing's broken, just bruised, but I could swear I see an odd expression play across his small face, half ashamed but pleased, despite the tears, as if he'd got what he wanted all along.

# What You Call Living

Is an animal that gets both shocked and stroked, and so puts up with the shocks, masochistic? Was Clara a masochist for putting up with Roy? She did some lay preaching and tricks on the side, wearing a T-shirt that read, "WHORES FOR CHRIST." Roy admired her for that. Prostitution may have its unsavory aspects, he knew, but sex isn't one of them. Clara belonged to that class of people who feel no pleasure when looking at the mirror, yet she still attracted men.

They met at the No Chance Saloon, trying a new alcoholic drink called Blur and abusing their short-term memories. The third time they encountered each other that evening, Roy declared, "Whenever I see you, I want to kill for you. Isn't that silly?"

Clara just smiled and made him feel several kinds of warm. "Everything in this climate draws blood." She pointed to her T-shirt. "See that stain? It's the color of sin."

He said, "I love your strange. Come sprong with me." She moved in with him the following week.

But Roy had a crackers-and-cheese mentality, though sometimes he thought it might be more thrilling to be a dwarf. He also had the mark of a child, which was to think he was fooling people when he wasn't. One Saturday evening, which Clara came to call The Night of the Stupid, Roy was in the bedroom, French-kissing her cat, when he remembered his dormant allergies. He quickly developed the sneeze and the cough, the wheeze and the itch.

Clara heard the noise and confronted them, all power concentrated into a snap of her fingers. "Scat, the two of you," she ordered. "I ought to have you both neutered." Roy was such a romantic that he missed her even before she left him. Eventually he became so contrite that he went down to the clinic and had his sexual organs altered. The operation seemed to quiet all allergic reactions, too. He called her and told her that he was a changed man.

"I said you ought to be fixed," said Clara, taken aback. "I didn't say I was right." Still, she returned, quelling the urge to charm someone new. Her tricks had dried up, anyway: most nights were like passing the hat around a graveyard.

It's been twenty years, and they're somewhat settled now. Roy will read aloud from the newspaper about scientists trying to grow fudge in a test tube. Clara is compiling a list of people who aren't fun anymore. They're on their third cat, who's getting stiff in the joints.

Once a week they take a late-night walk to see the stars, then ambivalently re-enter the house. Death is the old whisk broom in the closet. But there's got to be some way of getting beyond the sky.

# Portrait of Duff

When I think of Duff, I think of the itchiness of everyday life and the scratchiness of certain individuals. Duff wants to be loved for himself alone, but what's he got to offer? He's a one-man conversation with a personality like a sound-loop.

"Working on it," he answers, whether you're asking about his jottings, which he scrawls in a sixth-grader's spiral-bound notebook, or his constipation, which he throws a lot of prunes at. He writes while on the toilet so as not to waste time.

Mostly he doesn't care what he puts in his body—told me once he eats cream of meat. In fact, he's got an aversion to fancy food and the people who partake of it. When I invited him to a perfectly decent place called Café, he complained about high-concept restaurants with nowhere to sit and nothing to eat.

But I hang out with him because he's a thinker and shares his ideas. Like most great ruminators, he suffers from insomnia. The bomb in his head goes off at four every morning.

What does he jot down? "Transcendent moments," he told me, "like the silence after a burp or the pause just before a bird craps on the windshield." At my urging, he did try his hand at writing formal prose but got only as far as an essay title, "The Sadness of Warts."

Duff sneers at love. "These days, most women wouldn't, half of them aren't, and none of them do." But he's talked about sexing up someone he calls the fungus lady, whom he appreciates with tenderness and mayonnaise for her pleasing geometry.

Now that Duff's nearing sixty, he says he feels decaffeinated and often falls into what he calls a piece of forgetfulness. The routines he once swore by he now swears at, calling them exercises in daily futility. "It's all bananas from here on in," he mutters obscurely.

When he said he was on a roll, I didn't realize he meant downhill. But he still manages to get there and back. The other day I saw him with a blonde angel who was fondling his notebook and stroking his stubby pencil.

*What's your secret?* I want to nudge him. *Teach me your strategy!*

"Life is such a crap shoot," he smiles, loading the dice.

# Educating the Animals

Jill and I watched from the back-row bench as Charlie drove a whining electric car back and forth across the stage, finally exiting at a rakish left angle. After Charlie came Danny, who played basketball with a whiffle ball and a wire hoop, while Angie rode around him on a toy scooter. The manager, a bearlike woman in a faded brown sweater, kept up a cheerful patter: "*There* you go, Charlie. Round and round she goes, Angie. *That's* it, Danny—*very* good, sir!" Afterwards, the manager fed them Froot Loops with a measured hand. We slowly applauded, our claps echoing in the bare auditorium like someone being slapped. Since Charlie and Angie were cockatoos and Danny was a raccoon, the act was more impressive than if they'd been, say, retarded children, though it had the same air of exploitation.

Jill had the semi-hopeful look of someone who's reached a nadir and can expect better times ahead. We'd been in Hot Springs for two days and had run out of things to do the night before, when we'd eaten blackened alligator tail at a local restaurant. Jill hadn't liked it much, and I felt impelled to finish it, the way I always ate what remained of her salad or completed the tasks she grew tired of—sometimes she'd just leave the broom in the middle of a half-swept floor. Our three-year-old marriage was something neither of us had finished with, and this trip was our resuscitation attempt. Unfortunately, Jill got bored easily, and I became annoyed at her boredom.

202 | David Galef

Boredom, I insist, is a form of withdrawal. There is nothing inherently dull, only dull people. I'd raised this issue on more than one occasion, but Jill always got bored with the discussion.

So we looked around for something to do. Returning to the Tourist Information Center the next day, we both saw the pamphlet for the I.Q. Zoo at the same time: something cute with animals; that was all we could make of the fuzzy description. Jill shrugged like a cat, one shoulder higher than the other, which means she really can't decide and is hoping that I'll take responsibility. I figured we'd give it a try. Animals are easy to watch, right? But the I.Q. Zoo itself was hard to find: it wasn't at the street address listed, and when we inquired back at the Information Center, the silver-haired woman behind the desk said she had no idea.

"It probably doesn't exist anymore." Jill looked as if nothing quite existed anymore, which made me all the more determined. Half to get information and half to amuse her, I buttonholed the first five strangers and asked, but no one knew. Finally, an old bulldog of a policeman guarding the street corner told us it had moved to the edge of town, five miles out on Route 5.

Jill drove while I directed, but after a while we realized we must have missed something. We retraced the road slowly, unsure what to look for. Finally I spotted what had to be it, though it had changed its name. "EDUCATED ANIMALS," read the storefront sign in faded blue script, alongside a doll museum and a crystal shop. Jill looked at me; I looked at Jill. We nodded in unison and pulled up to the curb. Inside, the manager read a rolled-up newspaper with her arms folded above her broad midsection and barely looked up as we entered. She must have been in her mid-twenties, which was surprising since the population of Hot Springs seemed to be mostly senior citizens. This hadn't been immediately apparent, but when half the pedestrians walk with canes, and even the waitress at lunch has a silver perm, you get the idea. Jill was twenty-eight to my forty-five, though I tried to make up for it by acting childishly. Still, older people seemed to rattle her a bit. The seventy-year-old woman who ran our bed and breakfast told us that Florida retirees moved up to Arkansas when they found they missed the change of seasons. She didn't mention what they did once they got here, or maybe we could have followed suit. Most of them had that let-out-to-pasture look, suspecting an enclosure but roaming cautiously within its confines.

Once inside, we started looking at the store displays, mostly plastic and rubber animals. I wondered how I might secretly purchase a bright green rubber frog and slip it under Jill's pillow that night. "You folks here to see the show?" the manager asked.

Jill arched an eyebrow. "Why not?"

"Good," said the woman. "Next performance starts...in five minutes." She detached herself from the counter and moved over to the cash register. "That'll be two-fifty each."

Jill dug in her purse for the money, since last night's alligator special had been on me. We still kept our finances separate, but neither of us liked going dutch because it felt so tightwad, so we'd evolved a system that added up to the same thing without the fumbling awkwardness. She offered the woman a crumpled ten-dollar bill, which the woman tweaked from her hand as if it were a joke. After handing Jill back her change, she looked around us to see if anyone else would show up, and just then a mother led her two small sons into the store. They must have been about four and six, and they twisted in her grasp like toy balloons in a shifting wind. This was one of the reasons Jill never wanted children, and at times like that I thought she had a point. Did other species tug at its offspring that way?

"All right, all *right*," the mother told her children. "We're here, so behave now." She exchanged a glance of commiseration with the manager. She didn't make any eye contact with Jill, I noticed, probably because Jill looked feline and elegant. Aloof. This served her well for most occasions, though not so well down South, where we'd been traveling for over two weeks. When I told her this, she gave her standard response: "I have enough friends already."

204 | David Galef

The manager reached out to tousle the hair of the boys, both tow-headed and puppyish, as the mother paid for two children and one adult. From a roll of carnival-orange ADMIT ONE tickets, the manager tore off five, ripped those in half, and handed back a stub for everyone. "Follow me," she said, so we did: mother and children first, then Jill, then me.

Inside it was dark and grungy, with crumpled paper underfoot. The manager led us to the benches and stepped up on the stage. The first act wheeled out was a pair of macaws named General and Althea, with such brilliant lavender and blue plumage that it looked like the hair-coloring on some of the Hot Springs women. Their old-ivory beaks were curved and crafty, darting this way and that as if sensing invisible danger.

"These are genuine jungle macaws," the manager informed us, "with a starting price of three thousand dollars per pair. They can talk, fly at speeds of up to forty miles an hour, and have the intelligence of a three-year-old child. Show 'em how you can talk, General!"

General let out a terrible screech, frightening the younger of the two boys. The older boy roared back, which made Althea join in the screeching, and the manager had to distribute handfuls of Froot Loops to both birds and humans to get everyone to shut up. "Sorry 'bout that, folks—sometimes these bird-brains get a little out of hand. Have to be punished. In fact, we're gonna make an example of you, General—" and here she pulled out a dime-store pistol, pointed it at the bird, and cried, "Bang!"

General squawked and swung upside-down from his perch, one wing folded poetically over his breast.

"That's his John Wayne imitation," declared the manager. "He can do Hopalong Cassidy, too, when he's in the mood." Then she went on to the cockatoos and the raccoon, who seemed to get their routines mostly right, though with a decided lack of enthusiasm.

"Lack of motivation," murmured Jill. "That's what my fifth-grade teacher used to write on my report card." She would vouchsafe sudden confidences like that, half-explication, half complaint. I figured she was making herself vulnerable. I put my arm around her shoulder, and she sloped against my side. In front of us, the mother was telling her eldest to sit up straight.

The next acts were more complex. Lucky, a chocolate-and-white rabbit, sat down to tinkle a toy piano while a duck named Elvis played the guitar. "And this is Bertha our beauty queen," announced the manager, as an orange hen flapped open the door of her miniature henhouse and danced a jig to the mingled tunes. Bertha also leapt through a hoop. "That's it, *jump*—or you'll be a fried chicken," cackled the manager. After Bertha's last jump, the manager reached under Bertha and produced what she claimed was a chicken egg, though even in the poor lighting it was unmistakably a ping-pong ball.

It reminded me of a couple we knew, friends of Jill's, who had tried fertility drugs, artificial insemination, the whole bit. They finally adopted a Korean baby, but I couldn't help wondering what would happen as the kid grew up. Only a few species can be tricked into raising another's offspring. On the other hand, only humans ever opted to have no children at all. The very first night we made love, I figured the act itself without the consequences was all we'd ever want. Three years later, I wasn't so sure. I wrapped my arm around Jill's waist to pull her closer on the hard, backless bench as we watched the animals.

After the musical act, Lucky turned into a mathematician, adding and dividing numbers called out from the audience by tapping the right number on the keyboard. One plus two: three chords. Six divided by three: two chords. And so on. The younger boy couldn't get enough of this, dogmatically asking problem after problem. I thought of asking for three divided by zero as a way of ending the charade, but decided that Lucky probably had enough troubles as it was.

So I thought of other things, such as why we'd been attracted to Hot Springs in the first place. Like Rick in *Casablanca*, we'd come for the waters, and like Rick, we'd been misinformed. The hot-spring bathhouses had mostly shut down over a decade ago, victims of inflation and more scientific therapies. What remained was a historic bathhouse district, with a series of landmark buildings along Main Street. The striped awnings of the villa-esque structures still fluttered gently in the breeze, an eternal summer that our era had somehow eclipsed.

But the spa in the Majestic Hotel at the end of the block was still open. We went in mid afternoon when all the old folks were at the local horse races gambling with their social security checks. The lobby of the Majestic was the epitome of dilapidated elegance: scuffed gilt columns ringed by club chairs whose black leather had sprung from its studs, all overseen by a high ceiling fading into beige. An old woman lay asleep in one of the chairs, looking exactly like a comatose sheep, as a man determinedly vacuumed around her. When we asked the location of the baths, expecting some subterranean chamber, we were told to take the elevator to the third floor. There, for a surprisingly low price, Jill and I signed up for the full treatment, though it wasn't quite clear what that was. The facilities were separated by sex, so after leaving our valuables with the grandmotherly woman at the counter, we each walked in alone.

The inside was all decaying white tile and green-metal fixtures, built to accommodate a small school of health enthusiasts. According to Jill, who had studied the brochure, everyone from industrial magnates to gangsters had taken the waters here. I was handed a hospital gown by a bored-looking attendant named Eduardo and told to strip. Then he led me to a huge bathtub and began to run hot spring water into the tub. When the tub was full, he turned on the compressor, which began to agitate the water. I got a scrub with a loofah and was told to sit back and relax for a while. But the compressor's electrical switch was only a foot or so above the tub, and it was a while before I could dismiss the possibility of a nasty shock and look at something else. Accidents happen so easily, sometimes suddenly, sometimes over the course of years.

After twenty minutes in the tub, I was taken to an individual sauna stall, where I fantasized about being locked in and dying from dehydration. But Eduardo opened the door all too soon and led me to a table, where he swathed me with insolent skill in hot towels, then left me to unwrap a body five tables down. I felt as if I were being groomed for some unspecified function. About all I could do was to stare at the ceiling until it began, quite subtly, to stare back at me. The needle-shower was a relief, though with all its metal nozzles grouped in a metal cage it looked like a medieval torture device. By the time I was handed over to the masseur, I was pliant as a noodle. He was an old black man with a grip of iron, and he remarked as he kneaded me that he'd once been a horse handler. I wondered dimly what Jill was experiencing. I could rarely tell, even when she was doing exactly the same activity: eating the same food, sharing the same bed. Maybe we both lacked empathy or some other animal instinct.

I met Jill in the lobby as we'd arranged, both of us looking as if some giant hand had stuffed us back into our clothes. We'd both been—I don't know—manipulated, somehow rearranged in the baths, though Jill had managed to reapply her make-up. We sat in two of the club chairs for a while until I got the bright idea of ordering something to drink as a sort of reward for our ordeal. So we sat sipping gin and tonics and gazing at the hotel bar mural, which began with a pink waterfall just above a menagerie of jungle animals. They seemed to be watching us, or maybe the bartender as he puttered about the bar. The rest of the afternoon passed in the same slow motion.

A day later, my body was beginning to tense up again, but I could still feel the lingering touch of the masseur and the cleansing taste of gin. In the darkness in front of the stage, I involuntarily wriggled my shoulders, and Jill sat up startled. The older boy in front of us idly kicked the bench he sat on.

At the end of Lucky's calculations, we moved to the next room, with a series of booths in a half-circle. In the first booth, a hairy

pink pig drove a white plyboard Cadillac by pushing his snout at
an Erector-set steering wheel. The set of his jowls reminded me of
our heavyset neighbor, who happened to drive an '89 Coupe de
Ville. Next, a black Nubian goat rang a fire bell, at which point
a Bantam rooster acted as fire warden by walking along a wire to
pull an alarm. The cutest act—causing even Jill to coo—was last:
three yellow chicks climbed up a ladder to slide down a ramp into
a painted blue barrel of water, again and again until the music
stopped. It was all the mother could do to stop the younger boy
from joining them. In the end, she had to spank him as his brother
grinned.

We walked back through the entryway into the store, the mother chatting with the manager as we listened.

"Been here long?"

"Longer than most—about five years."

"Wants to know how she disciplines them so well," whispered
Jill in my ear.

"Shh."

The manager confessed that she'd started as the cashier out
front, then got enlisted to train. Right now business was slack,
but shows went on non-stop during the summer, and that required
four or five different groups of animals. "Most people sign on to
train figuring it'll be kind of fun, but they get tired of it after a
while and move on. They never learn."

"Where are the monkeys?" demanded the older boy.

"Sorry, we don't have any chimps around. They're too expensive." The manager shook her head as she casually scratched her
armpit. "But we used to do a lot of training for the circus when old
Miss Bailey ran the zoo. You can make big money that way. Fellow
called the Bird Man used to stop by twice a year and take some of
our feathered friends to Hollywood."

The younger boy had selected a rubber snake and was slowly,
rhythmically whipping it against the counter.

"Stop that, Billy. You stop that right now!"

This acted as a cue for Billy to do it all the harder, and the mother had to yank the snake away to get him to stop. Jill rolled her eyes in a manner I recognized all too well. I knew even then that this would be our last trip together. Should I have been more childish, should I have been more assertive? Where does intuition leave off and intelligence begin?

We left shortly afterward, exiting right after a woman in a rabbit costume came in. She obviously knew the manager, who greeted her as "Hare-Brain" and asked the boys if they'd like to sit on the lap of a big bunny rabbit. The last I saw of them, the younger boy was on the bunny's lap while his brother had hold of one furry ear, pulling it, stroking it, trying to make it his.